Match Wits with Super Sleuth Nancy Drew!

Collect the Original
Nancy Drew Mystery Stories®
by Carolyn Keene

Available in Hardcover!

Celebrate 60 Years with the World's Best Detective!

NANCY DREW MYSTERY STORIES®

The Haunted Showboat

BY CAROLYN KEENE

GROSSET & DUNLAP
Publishers • New York
A member of The Putnam & Grosset Group

PRINTED ON RECYCLED PAPER

Contents

'I think the cloaked pirate is Alex,' Nancy
whispered to Ned

CHAPTER I

The Stolen Car

"WOULD a trip to the Mardi Gras interest you, Nancy, and also a mystery to solve?" Bess Marvin asked.

Nancy Drew's blue eyes sparkled and her attractive face became animated. She gazed fondly at her two best friends who had just arrived and were seated in the Drew living room. Bess Marvin was blond and slightly plump. Her cousin, George Fayne, who had been given a boy's name, was an attractive brunette.

"Do you mean you're inviting me to go with you?" Nancy asked.

"That's right," George replied. "Our New Orleans relatives are extending an invitation not only to Bess and me, but also to the world's best girl detective!"

Nancy chuckled. "Thanks. What is the mystery about?"

"I don't know," Bess replied. "But they indicated in their letter that it must be solved by Mardi Gras time, which is not far off. You'll just love the Colonel and Aunt Stella."

"They have a daughter, haven't they?" Nancy asked.

Bess nodded. "Donna Mae is charming and pretty like her mother."

"But a bit spoiled," George added.

Bess explained that Donna Mae had formerly been engaged to a wonderful young man, named Charles Bartolome, who lived near the Havers outside of New Orleans. "But along came Alex Upgrove from New York and Donna Mae lost her heart to him completely. Their engagement is going to be announced the night of the big ball the Havers are giving at Mardi Gras time."

"It all sounds marvelous," said Nancy. "I accept the invitation!"

"Great!" Bess hugged her friend. "Before the ball, the Havers will put on a pageant of *The Sleeping Beauty*. The Havers will be king, queen, and princess. Afterward, they will greet their guests in these royal costumes."

"And I suppose," said George, "Alex Upgrove will be the prince."

Bess, still loyal to Donna Mae's former fiancé, said that Charles Bartolome had been invited to the ball, but had refused to attend.

"You can't blame him," said George dryly. "But he's being a good sport and not leaving a job he promised to do. Charles is in charge of restoring the showboat."

George explained that in a bayou on the Haver property was an old, abandoned showboat, the *River Princess*. "The Colonel is planning to have it brought to a dock on his estate. The ball will take place in the theater on the boat."

"Oh, it will be such an exciting trip," said Nancy enthusiastically. "Shall we drive to New Orleans in my car?"

"We'd love it," the cousins said in unison.

"When do you want to leave?" Nancy asked.

"As soon as possible," George replied. "The Colonel wrote that he wants to get the mystery cleared up 'right quick.'"

"I'll do my best," Nancy said eagerly.

Just then, the Drews' pleasant housekeeper came into the room. At once Nancy told her of the intriguing invitation.

Hannah Gruen smiled at the young detective. "So you're off on another case, Nancy. Well, I venture to say you won't return until you solve the mystery."

Middle-aged Hannah Gruen had lived with the Drews since the death of Nancy's mother many years before. She had acted as mother and counselor to the girl. Nancy, in turn, had a deep affection for Hannah.

"How do you plan to travel?" Mrs. Gruen asked.

When she heard the long trip was to be made in Nancy's blue convertible, Hannah looked dubious. "Are you going to do all the driving?"

"Oh, Bess and I will take turns," George spoke up.

Hannah looked relieved. But a moment later, as she gazed out the window, her face took on a worried look. "I'm afraid there's some snow in store," she said. "Oh, I do hope it holds off until you girls reach your destination."

"Don't worry, Hannah dear," said Nancy reassuringly. "We're all experienced drivers, and my faithful little car has gone through practically all kinds of weather."

Mrs. Gruen admitted this was true. "When will you girls be leaving?" she asked, a more cheerful expression on her face.

"Let's start the day after tomorrow," George suggested. "Bess and I are almost packed now. Is that enough time for you to get ready, Nancy?"

"Oh, yes."

After the cousins had left, Nancy telephoned her father, a prominent attorney in River Heights. When Mr. Drew heard about the Havers' invitation and the mystery Nancy was to solve, he said, "Go ahead by all means. This is a good opportunity to see New Orleans and you girls should have a wonderful time at the Mardi Gras."

The next day, Nancy and Hannah went over the girl's wardrobe and chose what they thought would be appropriate for the trip. Later, Nancy dashed downtown to buy a new skirt, blouse, and play suit to wear in New Orleans in case the weather should turn very warm.

When she returned, Nancy found the house-keeper inspecting a beautiful old black lace shawl and an intricately carved ivory fan. "I found these in a trunk in the attic," she said. "They belonged to your mother, Nancy. Wouldn't you like to use them at the ball, dear?"

"Oh, yes," Nancy agreed enthusiastically. "I'll get a costume to go with them."

Hannah Gruen left the room and Nancy laid the lovely old shawl on the bed. As she stood before the mirror, practicing how to use the fan, Togo, her little terrier, ran into the room.

"Hi, fellow!" Nancy said to the dog as she turned away from the mirror. The next moment she cried out, "Togo, bring that back! Drop it!"

The mischievous terrier had grabbed the shawl in his teeth and gone dashing up the hall with it. Nancy ran in pursuit and managed to get hold of Togo and the heirloom, but not before he had made a long tear in the lace.

"Oh, you naughty boy!" Nancy scolded.

The housekeeper came out of her bedroom and investigated the damage. "Don't worry,

Nancy, I think I can mend it so the tear won't show too much," she said soothingly.

An hour later Hannah Gruen brought the shawl to Nancy's room. The girl's eyes sparkled. "Why, I can't even tell where the rip was!" she exclaimed, planting a kiss on the housekeeper's cheek. "Thank you so much."

By evening Nancy's suitcase was packed and she put it in the luggage compartment of her convertible. With Togo at her heels, she locked the car doors, but left the garage open, since her father had not yet returned with his car.

A short time after Nancy and Hannah had gone upstairs again, Togo began to bark menacingly.

"I think I'd better go down and see what's bothering him," Nancy called to the housekeeper.

Nancy ran downstairs. As she reached the back door, she was thunderstruck to see her car being backed from the garage!

"Someone's stealing it!" Nancy gasped.

She hurriedly turned on the porch light, opened the door, and ran out to the driveway.

"Stop!" she called to the man at the wheel. "Stop!"

The driver, instead of slowing down, put on a burst of speed, swerving the rear of the car directly toward Nancy! The left fender grazed her, knocking her down! Then the driver straightened the wheels and the car roared off!

"Stop!" Nancy called to the man at the wheel

CHAPTER II

A Bomb Scare

HANNAH GRUEN had hurried downstairs. From the kitchen doorway she saw Nancy fall. With a cry of alarm she rushed from the house.

"Are you hurt?" the woman asked.

"It— The car just knocked the wind out of me for the moment," Nancy replied.

As Hannah helped Nancy to her feet, the girl looked mournfully down the street as the convertible disappeared around the corner.

"I'll call the police!" Hannah declared.

She and Nancy went into the house. The housekeeper urged Nancy to lie down for a few minutes, but the young detective insisted upon going to the phone herself.

"I can give the police a description of the car thief," she said. "He was dark and slender, with small, piercing black eyes. He had a very low forehead, and his hair looked coarse and stiff."

"That's an excellent description, Nancy," said the housekeeper. "I certainly hope the police catch him soon."

Before going to the phone, Nancy looked up the serial number of her car. Then she got in touch with Captain McGinnis of the River Heights police department.

After giving the thief's description, along with the car's serial and license plate numbers, Nancy recalled that her packed suitcase was in the car. She told the captain about this, then hung up.

"Oh, dear," she said to the housekeeper, "all my things are gone! I can get new clothes for myself, but I'd certainly hate to lose Mother's shawl and fan."

"I don't blame you, honey," said Mrs. Gruen. "But tell me this. How in the world could that man have taken the car? You locked it, didn't you?"

"Yes, I did. It means the man who stole it must be an experienced car thief."

Just then, they heard Mr. Drew's coupé come into the driveway. Nancy hurried to the kitchen door to meet her father, a tall, distinguished-looking man.

"What happened, Nancy?" Mr. Drew cried out, noting his daughter's disheveled appearance.

Quickly Nancy explained and Mr. Drew looked stern. "It's the work of an expert, all right. It wouldn't surprise me if the thief has a police record."

"That should make it easier to find him," said Nancy. She went back to the phone and called first Bess, then George at their homes. Both girls were aghast at the news and said they hoped the convertible, as well as Nancy's suitcase, would soon be recovered.

"I suppose we'll have to postpone the trip until we can make other arrangements," said Nancy. "I'll have Dad see if he can get us plane reservations in the morning."

"Oh, another day won't make any difference," said George. "Maybe by that time you'll have your car back."

But a phone call to the police department the next day was discouraging. Nancy's blue convertible had not been sighted on any road leading out of River Heights.

"We've made inquiries around town," said Captain McGinnis, "but so far my men haven't turned up a single lead."

During the morning Nancy shopped for new clothes to take on the trip. About five o'clock that afternoon Mr. Drew phoned his daughter to say that travel to New Orleans in Mardi Gras season was very heavy and it had been impossible for him to get plane tickets.

"But you're going just the same," he said.

"Call Bess and George and tell them to be ready tomorrow morning."

"But how are we traveling?" Nancy asked. There was no reply. Her father had hung up.

Nancy phoned her friends and gave them her father's message. "Dad has something up his sleeve," she said. "Maybe you'd better come over here and find out what's going on."

The cousins arrived in a short time and waited for Mr. Drew to come home. Presently a stunning new yellow convertible entered the Drews' driveway. Nancy's father, at the wheel, honked the horn loudly.

Nancy sprinted outside. Bess and George followed, bumping into each other to get to the car.

Mr. Drew wore a broad grin. "Like it, Nancy?" he asked.

"It's a beauty! Is it your new car and are you going to lend it to me, Dad?"

Mr. Drew stepped outside, made a low bow, and announced, "I'm going to do better than that. This car is yours!"

Nancy threw her arms around her father. "Oh, you're simply wonderful!" she exclaimed. "But what's going to happen if the police find my blue convertible?"

The lawyer said that he had arranged with the automobile dealer to take the blue car in trade if it should be recovered.

"I was thinking of turning it in, anyway," said Mr. Drew. "I was going to wait until your birthday and surprise you, but you sort of put one over on me by letting that thief take it!" he teased. Sobering, he went on, "That car had a lot of mileage on it and was showing wear."

"That's right," George spoke up. "And there was that big stain on the back of the rear seat where we upset an ink bottle and also a tear in the carpet."

Nancy chuckled. "Maybe that thief did me a favor," she remarked, then added wistfully, "But I certainly wish I could get my suitcase back."

As Bess and George said good-by, assuring Nancy that they would be ready early the following morning to start the trip to New Orleans, Mr. Drew turned to Nancy.

"How about taking the girls home in your new car?" he suggested. "After you drop them off, stop at police headquarters. Captain McGinnis wants you to look over the pictures in their rogues' gallery and see if you can identify the thief."

"Hop in, girls!" Nancy invited.

The three girls were thrilled with the smooth-riding quality of the yellow convertible and Nancy declared that driving it was no effort at all. After dropping the two girls at their homes, she continued on to headquarters. Here she looked at photograph after photograph of known car thieves.

"Not one of these," the young detective said finally, "looks like the man who stole my car."

"He may never have been apprehended," said Captain McGinnis. "Well, we'll keep up our search."

Nancy thanked him and went home. In order to keep her new car from being stolen, Mr. Drew had purchased a special padlock for one of the rear wheels. This was put on and the garage door locked.

The night passed uneventfully. In the morning, after breakfast, Mr. Drew carried Nancy's suitcase to the convertible. Then he and Hannah wished her a happy time on the trip and kissed her good-by.

"Thanks again, Dad," Nancy said as she waved and drove off.

A few minutes later she stopped at Bess's home, then at George's. All three girls wore smart wool dresses and warm car coats. The trio chatted gaily as they drove out of town, discussing the recent trip they had taken to Virginia, where Nancy and her friends had had many exciting adventures solving *The Hidden Window Mystery*.

"Speaking of mysteries," said George, "has there been any news of the car thief?"

"Not a clue," Nancy replied. "It's such a

beautiful day I think I'll take the back road through the country, instead of the highway, as far as Tartanville."

The road led through rolling farm land, where the houses were quite a distance apart. Nancy was driving just under the speed limit when the girls suddenly noticed a ticking sound coming from the dashboard.

"What's that?" Bess asked. "The electric clock? In a new car it shouldn't make that much noise."

Instantly Nancy pulled to the side of the road and turned off the ignition. She leaned down and looked up under the dashboard. Her face turned white with fear.

"There's an alarm clock taped on here!" she cried. "It may be the timer for a bomb! Girls, run as fast as you can! Stop anyone coming along!"

Bess and George dashed out the right-hand door, while Nancy reached down and shut off the alarm switch, hoping that would prevent the bomb from exploding. Then, for safety's sake, she got out and raced away from the car. Nancy ran in the opposite direction to the girls, in order to warn any oncoming motorist of possible danger.

Ten minutes passed. No one drove up and there was no explosion from Nancy's car. Finally George, making a megaphone of her hands, yelled to Nancy:

"What's next?"

Nancy called back that she was going to ask

the driver of the first car which appeared to go back to the next town and have someone sent out from the police force to remove the bomb.

Bess called, "How could anyone get into the car to plant a bomb with your garage locked?"

"The man probably jimmied open the garage window, and the car doors weren't locked."

As she finished speaking, Nancy became aware of a delivery truck approaching in her direction. She signaled the driver to stop, and told him her story.

"Golly!" The young man whistled. "Sure, I'll notify headquarters in a jiffy."

He turned and sped off. Twenty minutes later the girls were relieved to see a police car approaching.

"Thank goodness!" George exclaimed.

In a matter of seconds, a man wearing a mask, chest protector, and steel link gauntlets jumped from the car and opened the hood of the yellow convertible.

As the girls watched from a distance, the policeman lifted out a round object. There was no question but that it was a bomb! He dropped it into a bucket of oil before beckoning to the girls to come forward.

"What's back of this?" he asked.

Quickly Nancy explained what little she knew.

"Looks as if you have a pretty devilish enemy," the officer remarked.

"Yes," Nancy agreed.

Bess said, "He's a fiend trying to blow us up!"

"Well, his scheme was spoiled this time," the policeman said, and added, "Your car is okay now." He radioed a report of the incident to headquarters, then drove back to town.

The three girls stepped into the convertible and once more started off. As they entered the town of Tartanville, Nancy said she wanted to call her father and tell him what had happened. While she went into a drugstore to telephone, Bess and George waited in the car.

Just before Nancy returned, a man in a black convertible started to pass the cousins. He slowed down and stared first at Bess and George, then at the yellow car. Then the inquisitive man put on power and disappeared around a corner.

Suddenly Bess grabbed her cousin's arm. "George!" she cried. "That was Nancy's stolen car he was driving. It's been painted black!"

CHAPTER III

An Upsetting Delay

BY THE time George recovered from the surprise of hearing that the black automobile was Nancy's stolen car, the young detective herself had come from the drugstore.

"Quick! Jump in!" Bess urged.

Nancy instantly got behind the wheel of the yellow convertible. "What's up?" she asked.

"I saw your stolen car!" Bess told her. "The man drove it around that corner. Hurry!"

Driving as fast as she dared, Nancy headed in the direction her friend had indicated.

"It was painted black," Bess explained, "but I recognized the funny-shaped ink stain on the upholstery in the back seat."

"Say, that fellow could fit the description of the car thief," George spoke up. "I wish we had noticed the license number."

Nancy turned the corner and as she continued

down the street, the other two girls looked in every driveway and crossroad. But their quarry was not in sight.

After they had gone nearly a mile, Nancy stopped. "The thief had too much of a head start," she said. "Let's go back to police headquarters and report this."

As she was about to turn the car around, the girls saw a black convertible dart from an intersecting road some distance ahead and shoot down the highway.

"There he is!" Bess cried out.

Nancy set off in pursuit, but at the crossing was stopped by a red light. Irked by the delay, she put on extra power as soon as the traffic light turned green. The other vehicle was far ahead, but Nancy sped after it.

Suddenly George said, "Oh, oh!" as a motorcycle came roaring up behind them. In a moment it was alongside and the state trooper astride it motioned Nancy to the side of the road.

"Young lady," he said sternly, "don't you know what the speed limit here is?"

"Yes, sir, I do," Nancy replied, "but we're after a thief who stole another car of mine."

"Another car of yours?" The officer looked skeptical. "What kind of story is this?"

"It's true!" Bess spoke up earnestly. "Please help us catch the man who stole it."

"Well, okay. Follow me," the police officer directed.

By this time the black car was out of sight, but the trooper sped along with Nancy close behind. Two miles of country road were covered without the pursuers getting another glimpse of the suspect.

Finally, the state trooper stopped. He said that he would radio headquarters to set up a roadblock. The girls gave him a brief description of the black car and its driver. Then, taking a two-way radio from his pocket, the officer got in touch with his chief.

When he finished the radio report, the trooper turned to the girls. "Where are you from and where are you going?" he asked.

Nancy answered his questions, then added her theory that the same man might have planted the bomb. That would account for his stopping to look at the yellow convertible.

"We'll certainly try to find him," the trooper promised.

Nancy asked that the police get in touch with her father if they located the stolen car.

"And thank you for your help, officer. By the way, is there a short cut from here to Route 57?"

"Yes." The trooper gave directions and the three girls set off. As they rode along, Bess wore a worried frown.

"Oh, cheer up!" George chided her cousin.

"Don't feel bad because nothing came of your clue."

"It's not that," Bess answered. "Now that we've lost the thief, there's not a ghost of a chance of finding the car again. He knew that we were chasing him. And now he'll paint the convertible still another color."

George and Nancy agreed that Bess was probably right. "That isn't all there is to it, either," said Bess. "I have an awful feeling that thief doesn't want you to reach New Orleans, Nancy. He not only stole your blue convertible—he put a bomb in this car and now he's following us!"

"Even if that is true," George remarked, "what can we do?"

"Park this car in the next town and go to New Orleans by train," Bess declared.

There was silence for several seconds, then Nancy said reassuringly, "Oh, Bess, we won't have to do that. If the thief stops to have the car repainted, we'll get there way ahead of him."

Bess thought this over, then felt better. "Well, all right," she said. "But let's step on it!"

Presently Nancy pulled to the side of the road. "Your turn at the wheel," she said to George, who nodded and changed places with her friend.

Half an hour later they came to the bustling little town of Wrightsville.

"Oh, look!" Bess called out. "There's a showroom with the same make car as this one. Isn't that green sedan in the window a beauty?"

"It certainly is," Nancy agreed. "But I'd rather have this yellow convertible."

George had gone only half a block farther when suddenly the new car developed a strange, grinding noise in the rear.

Bess groaned. "Now what?" she asked.

Nancy was frowning. She suggested that George go around the block and come back to the service station connected to the automobile showroom. George turned at the next corner, but had not gone far when the noise grew definitely louder.

"We'd better stop," Nancy advised.

As George pulled toward the curb, it sounded as if the rear end of the car had dropped to the street! Quickly the girls jumped out and rushed back to look. Nancy knelt to peer underneath.

"Oh, no!" she exclaimed in a woebegone voice. "The whole rear housing has given way!"

Nancy rose and for several seconds the three girls stared questioningly at one another. Was this a mechanical failure? Or had Nancy's enemy tampered with the housing, in case the bomb failed to go off?

"I'll walk back to that service station and have the car towed in," said Nancy. "You stay here and guard our baggage."

Although Nancy tried to sound nonchalant, Bess and George knew she was extremely upset.

"This is a shame!" George declared angrily, after Nancy had left.

"And dangerous!" Bess added. "If we'd been out on the highway going fast, we might have been killed!"

In a few minutes a tow car arrived and the disabled convertible was hoisted up and pulled to the service station. The three girls watched as the mechanics examined the broken housing. Presently one of them walked off to his workbench.

He searched for several seconds among his tools, then picked up a small leather case. From it he took a magnifying glass. Holding this in one hand and a strong flashlight in the other, he made a thorough investigation of the metal section where the break had taken place.

Finally he turned to Nancy. "This wasn't any mechanical defect," he announced. "I'd say someone poured acid on the housing!"

The girls were aghast, but there was no question in their minds as to who had been responsible. Either the man who had stolen her car, or an accomplice, had damaged the new convertible.

"I'll get the boss," the mechanic offered. "He'll see what can be done."

The owner, Dan Compton, was summoned

from the showroom. He examined the damage and agreed with the mechanic.

"This is certainly bad luck for you girls," Dan said. "Where was this car purchased?"

When Nancy told him, he nodded. "Oh, I know Harry Smith in River Heights. He's a good friend of mine." After a moment he added, "I'll phone him, and we'll work something out."

Without giving Nancy a chance to comment, he hurried to his office and put in the call. Five minutes later he returned to the garage, a smile on his face.

"Everything's arranged, Miss Drew," he said. "Harry wants me to lend you a car. I'm going on a little vacation and the car I ordinarily use for demonstrations will be idle. You're welcome to take it for your trip. By the time you come back this way, your convertible will have a new housing in it."

Nancy's face broke into a broad grin. "I certainly appreciate your help," she said.

"Of course my demonstration car is not so fancy as yours," Dan Compton told her. "It's black, and the upholstery is just plain dark green."

He led them to a corner of the garage where the car stood. Bess smiled. "This suits me much better. The car is dark and inconspicuous. Now maybe that awful man won't notice us."

Before leaving town, the girls ate a belated

lunch. Then they started off once more. By evening Bess was driving and the girls began to discuss how much farther they would go before stopping for the night.

"There's an attractive motel, The Cedars, about two miles from here," George said. "A neighbor of ours stopped there on a trip recently."

"Let's go there," Bess put in. "I'm starved!"

Nancy glanced at her watch. It was nearly seven o'clock and she, too, was getting hungry. "I vote we stay at the motel tonight."

When they reached The Cedars, Bess turned in and parked. After the girls had been assigned to modern, comfortable rooms, they washed, brushed their hair, then went to a coffee shop next to the lobby.

"Mm. I'll have this fried chicken platter," Bess decided as she studied the menu.

"Sounds wonderful to me," Nancy said, and George chose the same.

Then Nancy asked the girls to order for her. "I want to phone home and tell Dad about the sabotaged housing."

When the connection was made with her home, Hannah Gruen answered.

"Hello, Hannah! How are you and Dad?"

"Oh, we're fine," said Hannah. "We have some news for you."

"Yes? What is it?" Nancy asked eagerly.

"Your stolen license plates were found."

The housekeeper said that the River Heights police had had a tip from a disgruntled hoodlum who had been promised some money by a man and never been paid.

"So this fellow decided to talk," Mrs. Gruen explained. "He told the police about a deserted cabin outside of town where some car thieves had dumped stolen license plates. The ones from your car, Nancy, were among them."

"Oh!" said Nancy.

Mrs. Gruen went on, "And—and they found something else, too. Oh, Nancy, you *must* be careful!"

CHAPTER IV

A Nerve-Tingling Ride

"MAYBE you girls had better give up the trip," Mrs. Gruen suggested nervously.

"But why?" Nancy asked. "What else *did* the police discover?"

The housekeeper said that among the pile of stolen plates which had been found there was a pistol. Apparently it had been accidentally dropped. Hannah was sure that a dangerous person or persons who carried weapons intended to make trouble for Nancy, Bess, and George if they continued their trip.

Nancy herself was worried, and told Hannah what had happened to the new car. But she added quickly:

"We're driving a different car. It's black, and not so conspicuous as the yellow one. What's more, we saw the thief. Now that he knows he's been recognized, he won't dare appear in the daytime. Please don't worry, Hannah dear."

"Well, I suppose it's all right," said the housekeeper. "I do wish your father were here to advise you. But he's gone out of town for the night."

Nancy said good-by and hung up. When she relayed the latest clue to Bess and George, they agreed that the safest thing for them to do would be to get ahead of the thief on the road.

"So let's start at once," said Nancy, "and drive until dawn at least. We can take turns driving and sleeping. Suppose we eat supper here. Then we'll give up our rooms and start on."

The girls found the meal of fried chicken, accompanied by hot corn bread and sweet potatoes, very tasty. For dessert they had delicious homemade pecan pie.

"I could go to sleep right now," said Bess, yawning contentedly. "I ate too much!"

"I feel fine," George said. "I'll take first turn at the wheel."

After picking up their bags, the girls went to the car. Nancy and Bess climbed into the rear seat and were soon sound asleep. George drove for nearly two hours, then stopped. She awoke Bess, who was to take her turn at driving.

"Where are we?" asked the plump girl, sleepily surveying the blackness around them.

George said they had crossed the state line a half hour ago. "We're getting into the mountains now, so take it easy," she advised.

As Bess started off, she was very quiet. She did not reveal her feelings to her cousin, but she was beginning to think that the trip had a jinx on it.

The wind was blowing hard, there was no moon and not one star in the sky. Bess felt a slight chill run up her spine.

"It's just plain spooky!" she told herself.

By now, George was sleeping soundly beside Nancy in the rear seat. Bess, a good driver, put mile after mile behind them. Fortunately, there was only one main road, so she had no decision to make about which direction to take. But at one o'clock she came to an intersecting highway.

"Now which way do I go?" Bess asked herself, stopping the car.

Turning her spotlight on the sign, she carefully read the names of the towns in each direction. Not one of them was familiar to her and gave her no clue as to which road to take. Bess opened the glove compartment and took out a map. She spread it on her lap and tried to figure out just where she was.

Suddenly a voice at her elbow startled her, "Can I help you?"

Alongside her partially open window stood a smiling young man. Bess gave an involuntary squeal, then asked, "Wh-where did you come from?"

Her outcry had awakened the two girls in the rear seat. They sat up, alert at once. Both were amazed to see the stranger.

"Hello there," he said pleasantly to Nancy and George. To Bess he added, "I see you have passengers."

"Yes," said Bess. "And maybe you *can* help us."

"Glad to," the young man replied. "Sorry if I frightened you. I just parked over in those woods with my trailer about half an hour ago and hadn't gone to bed yet. When I saw you stop, I figured you might be lost. Where do you want to go?"

"New Orleans," Bess replied.

The young man laughed. "You're a long way from there," he said. "But at this point I think the best thing for you to do is turn left, go through Titusville, and then hit the highway."

"Thank you very much," Bess said with a smile.

She was already folding up the map and putting it away. As she started off, the stranger called, "Oh, wait a minute!"

Bess instantly became alarmed. Was this man going to detain them? But he went on pleasantly, "Say, maybe you're the three girls that man was asking about a little while ago."

"What man?" Nancy spoke up quickly.

"A fellow in a black convertible with black-and-red seat covers. He stopped here right after I parked and I came out to talk to him. He asked me if three girls traveling alone had gone past here."

Nancy and her friends looked questioningly at one another. Could the driver have been the person who had stolen Nancy's car?

"Oh, I'm sure we're not the girls he meant," George put in hastily. "What did this man look like?"

The description the stranger gave exactly fitted that of the car thief!

"What else did he say?" Nancy asked.

"The man said that the two cars had been traveling together, but somehow had become separated."

"I see," said Nancy. "Did he happen to say where he was going?"

"No, he didn't."

"Which road did he take?"

The young man pointed straight ahead. Bess asked, "Could you go to New Orleans taking that road?"

"Yes, you could. It would be shorter, as a matter of fact. But the road isn't very good."

Nancy asked to see the map and once more Bess took it out of the compartment. A thought had come to the girl detective—maybe the affable young stranger was in league with the car thief!

Although she realized her suspicions probably were wrong, Nancy decided it would be best not to take either of the roads he had mentioned.

Following her hunch, she told him briefly that the girls had had enough driving for one night and would stay at a hotel in the nearest town.

"Turn right, Bess," she said.

She thanked the young man for his help, then the girls drove off. Nancy told the cousins her suspicions and said that as soon as they reached another crossroad, they would turn left. "Then we'll go left again and finally hit Titusville."

She and George kept looking out the rear window to see if any car was following them but they saw none.

Finally Nancy said, "We're safe so far."

Soon she took her turn at the wheel. Nancy wondered who was ahead in the race to New Orleans—the girls or the car thief. Hopefully she thought:

"If that young man at the crossroads was honest, and not in league with the driver of the black car, maybe we have outwitted the thief!"

Beginning to feel weary, Nancy decided they had better stop at a motel. Just beyond the small town of Titusville, she came to an attractive one and turned in. As she pulled into the well-lighted parking area, the young detective's eyes widened.

Next to her stood a black convertible with new-looking black-and-red seat covers!

Nancy quickly woke Bess and George, told them where they were, and pointed to the car. "Look!" she said excitedly.

Bess gave a shiver. "You mean we're about to close in on the car thief? Shouldn't we notify the police and let them do it?"

Nancy said that she was going to consult the motel proprietor first as to who was driving the car. The three girls took their bags from the luggage compartment and walked into the office of the motel. A plump, bald-headed man sat in a barrel-shaped chair, his head resting on his chest. He was snoring slightly.

Nancy walked up and tapped the man on the shoulder. He awoke with a start. "You want rooms?" he asked sleepily.

Nancy nodded, then said, "Would you mind telling me who the person is that came here in the black convertible with red-and-black seat covers. We're looking for someone with a car like that."

"Person!" the plump man exploded. "You mean that gang! Mother, father, three children, a dog, a cat, and a parrot!"

The three girls burst into laughter. "Wrong family!" Nancy chuckled. "Well, have you two nice rooms for us?"

The proprietor took the girls' bags, and his

keys, leading the way down a corridor. "These are the best accommodations we have," he said, smiling, and unlocking adjoining rooms. "Oh, I was so sleepy I forgot to ask you to register."

"We'll do it in the morning," said Nancy.

She preferred this arrangement, just in case the car thief might arrive later at the motel and learn from the proprietor that the girls were there.

The girls slept soundly, but were wide awake by seven o'clock. Bess, the first to look outdoors, groaned.

"Snow!" she exclaimed. "A regular blizzard!" Bess suggested that they delay their trip, at least for a day.

But by the time the girls had eaten breakfast, the snowfall had slackened and Nancy decided it would be safe for them to go on. She herself took the wheel, with her two friends in front with her. They had not gone many miles when they came to a roadblock with a huge sign indicating a detour to the right.

"Goodness only knows what's ahead of us," Bess said nervously.

Nancy turned. Half a mile farther on, the road led up a steep incline. As the girls neared the summit of the hill, they saw that there was a sheer drop to the left of the road.

"Oh, do be careful!" Bess begged.

"Hush!" George commanded.

Although Nancy was sure that the tires were excellent, she would be relieved when the car had safely reached the bottom of the hill on the other side.

Nancy reached the summit and was just about to start down the steep incline when all three girls gasped at the frightening sight which confronted them.

"Oh!" Bess screamed. "Stop!"

Across the road ahead lay two sections of an electrical cable which had been snapped by the storm. Sparks flashed dangerously from the broken ends!

Nancy put on her brakes. The next instant the car skidded toward the left of the road with its sheer drop of thirty feet!

CHAPTER V

The Mystery at Sunnymead

As THE tires sank into the snow three feet from the edge of the cliff, the car miraculously held the road. Hastily the three girls scrambled out.

After several seconds had elapsed, and the car still held its position, Nancy said, "I guess it's not going to move."

At that moment snow started to fall again. The girls pulled their coat collars tightly around their necks and glanced up the road. The live wires continued to sparkle and crackle.

"This is really a predicament!" George declared.

"It certainly is," Nancy agreed. "We couldn't possibly continue on the road, even if I dared to try moving the car."

"That's right," said George. "If these rear wheels spin, the car may go over the cliff."

"What will we do?" Bess asked nervously. "Hike to the nearest house?"

"I hope not," George said quickly. "It must be three miles back."

Nancy walked to the rear of the car and looked down the embankment. "There's one thing we can try," she said thoughtfully.

"Not with us inside the car!" Bess stated flatly.

"No. Fortunately, the rear of the sedan is a few feet from the edge of the cliff. If we could just move the car back onto the road, I could back down the hill."

"But how in the world can you move the car back onto the road without driving it?" Bess asked.

Nancy said that one time when she was trying to squeeze onto a ferryboat with her car she had found it impossible to steer into position. Two men had jolted the rear of the vehicle up and down until it actually bounced off the ground. Then they had quickly lifted it a few feet to one side.

"So three girls ought to be able to do the same thing now," she said.

Bess still looked dubious but George was willing to try it. She insisted, however, that they first block the front wheels with stones so there would be no chance of the car rolling back on them.

"Good idea," Nancy agreed.

The girls kicked at the piles of snow along the side of the road until they found two substantial rocks. These were pushed securely behind the front tires. Then the three friends took positions behind the sedan.

"I'll count," said Nancy. "When I say 'three,' heave ho!"

Leaning over, they grasped the bumper and began to jounce the car up and down. The girls' faces were strained as they waited for a high bounce.

In a moment Nancy said, "One! Two!" Bess and George worked feverishly, then waited. "Three!" Nancy cried.

Together the girls lifted the rear of the car almost two feet back toward the center of the road.

"Hypers!" cried George, using her favorite expletive. "It worked. Nancy, you're a brain child!"

Nancy stepped into the car and started the motor. She drove forward a few inches, so that Bess and George could remove the stone blocks. Then they too climbed in.

Slowly Nancy began to back down the hill. This proved to be difficult to do, because the wind had shifted and blown quantities of the snow across the road. Twice the car stuck fast and the cousins had to get out and tramp down the drifts before she could proceed.

Finally Nancy reached the foot of the hill. She consulted the map again and turned to the right. Half an hour later they came to the main highway.

Suddenly Bess said apprehensively, "I only hope that car thief is holed up somewhere because of the storm."

"I have a hunch he is," Nancy said cheerfully.

Toward the end of the day the girls left the snowstorm behind. To make up for lost time, they drove until eleven that night before they stopped at a motel. By this time they had reached Alabama, with its blooming plants, green grass, and beautiful trees.

"What a relief this scenery is!" said Bess, getting out of the car and stretching.

"And the temperature," George added. "It was only ten degrees when we left. Now it's about sixty!"

After a good night's sleep and a hearty breakfast the next morning, the girls started off again. Soon they were in an area of lovely Southern plantations. They were thrilled by glimpses of the homes, so large and stately with their tall columned porches and beautiful gardens. Quaint cabins, formerly used by slaves, stood some distance away from the houses.

Bess ohed and ahed to such an extent that George finally said teasingly, "You remind me of a dripping ice-cream cone, Bess. Sweet, but oh so gooey!"

"I wish," Bess retorted, "that you could enjoy it the way I do."

Nancy, to change the subject, said, "Tell me about your cousin Donna Mae."

"Well," Bess began, "she's a year older than I am, tall and pretty. She has blond hair and great big blue eyes."

George interrupted laughingly, "And does she roll those eyes around to get her own way!"

"You're just jealous," Bess told her. "Any girl who could be engaged to two men in one year—"

George tossed her bobbed head at the remark. "One would be enough for me! But really, I've always liked Donna Mae. I wonder why she broke her first engagement. There must have been a serious reason."

"Or just a change of heart." Nancy remarked.

The rest of the trip was one of banter and teasing, and exclamations, even by George, over the beauty of the scenery. The car thief was almost completely forgotten.

"I've never seen such exquisite azaleas in my life!" Bess remarked, as the girls drove through the Mobile area.

"As I recall," said Nancy, "this place is noted for its azaleas."

"Yes, it is," Bess replied. "The Garden Clubs put on special tours for tourists to see them."

"But this ride," joked George, "is a privately conducted tour by Drew and Company!"

Soon the girls reached the broad Mississippi and gazed at the peaceful, somewhat muddy river.

"It looks harmless enough, doesn't it?" George remarked. "But think of the pirate days when travelers weren't safe on it!"

Nancy followed the river road for several miles, then turned inland.

"Sunnymead is just ahead," Bess announced.

Five minutes later the car turned into a long driveway edged with live-oak trees. At the end of it stood a square Colonial mansion. It was painted yellow, and white columns reached from the ground to the roof. Two stories of porches ran around the entire building.

As the girls reached the house, George leaned over and blew the horn. Donna Mae, wearing a low-necked bouffant dress, rushed out to greet the visitors.

"You're really here!" she cried joyously. "You all had me so worried when I kept hearing of your delays."

Behind her was Mrs. Haver, an older yet charming version of Donna Mae. She wore an attractive blue linen dress.

"Welcome to Sunnymead!" Mrs. Haver exclaimed with a gracious smile.

In back of her walked Colonel Haver, a tall, erect man of fifty with twinkling blue eyes and black hair slightly gray at the temples.

Nancy was introduced to the family. Then she said, getting out of the car, "I'm afraid I shall have to take all the blame for our being late in arriving. A little unsolved mystery overtook us."

"Yes," Bess added, "Nancy's beautiful car was stolen and we were playing hide-and-seek with the thief." She quickly told all that had happened.

"Oh, how perfectly ghastly!" Donna Mae exclaimed. "Didn't you almost die?"

"Well, it wasn't any fun," George agreed.

A moment later an elderly colored couple, wearing a maid's and a butler's uniforms, came from the house. They were introduced as Mammy Matilda and Pappy Cole. The two smiled pleasantly. Then, as Pappy Cole started to unload the car, Mammy Matilda said to the visitors:

"I sure hopes you all have a fine time durin' your visit here."

"Thank you," said Nancy. "I'm looking forward to it." Turning to Colonel and Mrs. Haver, she added, "It's certainly most kind of you to invite me."

Mrs. Haver smiled. "The pleasure is ours. We're always delighted to have friends of Bess and George visit us."

A young man came from the house and joined the group. He was proudly introduced by Donna Mae as Alex Upgrove.

"I'm charmed," he said to the visitors in a clipped, well-modulated voice.

The River Heights girls shook hands with the slim, brown-haired young man. Nancy instantly decided that he might be termed handsome, but Alex had an air of superiority which spoiled the first impression.

A few minutes later Mammy Matilda served tea in a patio at the rear of the house. It overlooked one of the most exquisitely beautiful gardens Nancy had ever seen. Flowering cherry and plum trees served as a colorful background for beds of various colored roses, azaleas, and camellias.

In choosing seats on the patio Alex found one next to Nancy and at once engaged her in conversation. Bess brought up the subject of the car thief and said that in her opinion the man had been trying to keep the girls from coming to New Orleans.

"Oh, I don't see how that could possibly have any bearing on your trip here," Alex declared. "And surely you have no idea there is any connection between this thief and the mystery at Sunnymead, have you?"

George replied. "Yes, we do. But I hope we're wrong."

Alex laughed, then as the conversation became more general he leaned toward Nancy and whispered:

"You and I are going to have a wonderful time together solving the plantation mystery!"

Nancy was startled. She thought the remark most inappropriate, in view of the fact that Alex's engagement to Donna Mae was to be announced soon.

Pretending that she had misunderstood Alex, she said, "Yes, I want you and Donna Mae to tell me all the details when you have a chance."

A look of annoyance came over Alex's face. "Of course," he muttered. "Any time."

When the tea hour was over, the four girls went upstairs. As Mammy Matilda helped the visitors unpack, Donna Mae talked incessantly about her fiancé.

"Isn't he a darling?" she asked, "And smart, too. You know, Alex is a graduate of Oxford University in England! And he's fabulously wealthy—not that that makes any difference to me. But his family is simply wonderful—socially prominent, you know."

A look of surprise came over George's face, for she had never before thought Donna Mae snobbish. "Have you met them?" she asked.

"Oh, no, but they wrote me a simply darling letter from Paris and called me their new daughter. I'll meet them sometime soon."

Donna Mae explained that her father had looked up the Upgrove family. At the present time they were all in Europe.

"You must see his college pictures," she babbled on. "He has them with him."

"Donna Mae," George asked abruptly, "what happened between you and Charles Bartolome?"

Instantly Donna Mae sobered. "We—we—had a falling out on account of Alex. I met Alex while Charles was away on a long trip—and we became friends. But Charles didn't approve, and I got annoyed with his possessiveness. So I broke off my engagement to him."

She hesitated. "To tell you the truth my conscience hurt me for a while. I shouldn't have dated Alex but I was lonely. And Alex was so wonderful to me. He's a more aggressive type than Charles, and he's *so* in love with me. I wonder where he is now!"

As if she could not bear to stay away from him a moment longer, Donna Mae said, "See you later! I have to talk to Alex," and hurried out of the room.

Bess looked at the other girls and shook her head. "I've never seen a bigger change in anyone. Have you, George? Donna Mae just isn't like her old self."

"You're right, Bess," replied her cousin, "and I wouldn't say for the better. Maybe it's Alex's influence."

After dinner that evening Colonel Haver took Nancy aside. "I'd like you to get started solving the mystery as soon as possible," he said. "Time is running out."

He explained that stories of strange happenings on the showboat had caused workmen to refuse to go near it.

"Not a single towboat captain will come here to push the *River Princess* out of the bayou. We must do something fast!" He smiled and added, "Are you ready to take over, Detective Drew?"

CHAPTER VI

Pirates' Alley

GIVING the Colonel a big smile, Nancy said excitedly, "I'd like to start solving the mystery at once."

"Fine," he replied. "And there's one thing I want to say. You'll have free rein. Don't feel obligated to report to me or to anyone else. Come and go as you like."

Nancy was glad to hear this. The following morning she went into the garden to gaze at the bayou which lay beyond the extensive flower beds. Large water oaks, dripping with long festoons of Spanish moss, rose above the mist which covered the swamp. Eerie clumps of cypress and gum trees could be seen against the sky.

Nancy could not restrain a little shiver. "That's the swamp we must go through to reach the showboat," the young detective murmured to herself.

Her thoughts were interrupted by the arrival of Donna Mae. With a charming smile, she said,

"Good mornin', honey. Hope you slept well!" Then, following Nancy's glance, she added, "That old place is positively spooky, isn't it? Don't think about it! We're going to New Orleans and have some fun."

"But, Donna Mae, I have some work to do for your father," Nancy protested.

Donna Mae made a face. "Work! Who wants to work at Mardi Gras time?" she asked gaily. "You know, you're going to be in the play we're having just before the ball and you must get a costume at once. Alex is going to drive all of us girls to town. We'll show you some interesting sights in the old city."

The planned excursion sounded most attractive and Nancy brushed aside her serious mood. "You're right, Donna Mae," she said. "New Orleans *is* such a famous place. Of course I want to see it. I can start my sleuthing later. A few hours won't matter, I guess."

"Wonderful! We'll start at ten o'clock," Donna Mae said. "I'll tell Bess and George."

At ten Alex drove to the front door in a station wagon. When the girls from River Heights came out they wore pastel summer cottons.

"How pretty you all look!" Alex remarked as he alighted to help the girls in. Then to Nancy, who stood to one side, he whispered, "Please sit next to me. I want to talk to you about the mystery."

"Oh, there's plenty of time for that," Nancy replied coolly, ignoring the invitation. "Donna Mae just wants us to have fun today." She deliberately climbed into the rear seat, where Bess and George would sit.

As they neared the city, Donna Mae, next to Alex, directed him to a fine old street in the residential area. She asked him to stop in front of a two-story, balconied yellow house. The property was surrounded by a wrought-iron fence with an oleander pattern. In the garden beyond were several magnolia trees and oleander bushes. Bess gave a sigh of admiration.

"The oleander blossom," Donna Mae explained, "is the city flower of New Orleans. The juice of the bush itself is poisonous, you know."

"Why are we stopping here?" Alex asked her.

"Madame Dupre, who lives here, rents costumes for the Mardi Gras," Donna Mae replied. "Her selection is exceptional and the costumes unique."

Alex decided to remain in the car while the girls went inside. It took only a few minutes to choose their costumes. At Donna Mae's insistence her friends would represent fairies in the play. They would wear white, fluffy tulle ballet dresses with wings attached. George grumbled that she was going to feel very silly in hers.

"I hardly think I rate wings, anyway!" she

said wryly. "And the costume reminds me of dancing school when I was four years old!"

Donna Mae had her way, however. The costumes were packed and the girls walked outside with the boxes. To their amazement Alex and the station wagon were not in sight.

"Now where did he go?" asked Donna Mae, annoyed.

Minutes later Alex returned and explained that he had been doing some sight-seeing while waiting for them.

"We'll tour the old city first," said Donna Mae, "and then lunch at Antoine's."

The Vieux Carré, or old city, was nestled on the east bank of the Mississippi. The modern city of New Orleans spread beyond it for some distance. Alex parked and the tour began on foot.

The visitors were intrigued by the narrow streets and sidewalks, the ancient shops and restaurants, and the homes with their heavy wooden doors and iron hinges and locks.

The two- and three-story buildings looked delightfully quaint with their lovely wrought-iron railings. Boxes of bright-colored flowers dotted the porches. Here and there were open gates leading to charming old-fashioned courtyards.

"Visitors are welcome to walk in and look around," Donna Mae announced as she led the way into one of the gardens.

"Oh, how artistic!" Bess exclaimed.

The flagstone courtyard was decorated with tubs of flowering bushes in full bloom. In the center a fountain played and at the far side a curved stone stairway led upward to a flower-decked balcony. The warm tropical sunshine lent an air of tranquility to the scene.

"It's heavenly, simply heavenly!" Bess sighed.

As the sight-seers left the quaint spot, Donna Mae said, "Nancy, you and the girls will surely want to see the haunted house. It's famous in this area."

"What makes it haunted?" Bess asked quickly.

"Well," began Donna Mae, "a long, long time ago there was a fire in the old house. The owner and his wife were not there when it happened, so firemen and neighbors broke in and saved what furniture they could. To their horror they found slaves chained in the attic.

"When the owner and his wife heard that their dreadful cruelty had been discovered, they ran away. But it's said that the ghosts of those slaves haunt the place."

"I don't think I want to see that house," Bess said with a shudder.

Alex suggested that probably they would be more interested in the pirates, anyway. To Donna Mae, he said, "How about showing the girls the place where Pierre Lafitte was a prisoner?"

Donna Mae led the way to Jackson Square, the heart of the Vieux Carré. In the center of this grassy esplanade stood a statue of Andrew Jackson, the seventh president of the United States. The general sat astride a rearing horse.

When George remarked that it was amazing how the forelegs of the horse remained in space with no support, Donna Mae said that this had been accomplished by making the statue perfectly balanced. "An unusual and difficult feat in this case."

Donna Mae went on, "The government of New Orleans has been in the hands of different ruling groups five times. Sometimes it was the Spanish, sometimes the French, sometimes the United States, and once the city was independent."

Around Jackson Square were numerous public buildings and apartment houses. Alex, who had been on the tour before, led the way to the *Cabildo*. This large, many-arched building had originally been the municipal hall for old New Orleans. Now it was a museum.

Off the center courtyard around which the *Cabildo* had been built was the small cell in which Pierre Lafitte, the pirate, had been jailed. At the moment there was little in it—the most interesting objects being two ancient safes with decorated crosspieces of a hobnailed design.

"Are these what the pirates kept their gold in?" George asked with a twinkle in her eyes.

"So the legend goes," Donna Mae answered. "Pierre and his brother Jean had a blacksmith shop a few blocks from here. They didn't do much blacksmithing, though. They were too busy smuggling in slaves from Africa and selling them.

"Jean and Pierre Lafitte were in trouble with the law most of the time," Donna Mae continued, "but somehow, they were always able to get out of it. But, strange though it seems, they turned out to be very patriotic citizens during the War of 1812 in the Battle of New Orleans."

"Well, I'm glad they made up for their miserable deeds," said Bess.

"Let's walk up Pirates' Alley," Alex suggested. "That's the street where the pirates carried on their nefarious schemes."

As the group walked across Jackson Square to Pirates' Alley, the girls became interested in the many sidewalk artists. The men and women lined one side of the square. Many wore smocks and jaunty berets. Some sat on stools, sketching portraits of tourists, and all had pictures on display to sell.

One aggressive man smiled at Nancy, "May I paint your portrait, miss?" he asked. "Your face would be lovely on canvas!"

Nancy laughed. "Not today, thank you," she answered.

Alex led the way into the narrow street nick-

named Pirates' Alley. It was so attractive, with
its quaint architecture and flowering plants, that
it was hard for the girls to think of sinister plans
once being made there by scheming pirates.

Just as the sight-seers emerged from the alley,
Nancy grabbed George's arm. "I just turned
around and saw a man who looks exactly like the
one who stole my car! He must be following us!"

George suggested getting a policeman, but
Nancy said, "No. I'd like to follow him if possible. We may learn something. Suppose you
and Bess and I duck into the first antique store
we come to and let him pass us."

George whispered directions to Bess, as Nancy
glanced over her shoulder to be sure the man was
still following. He was!

Coming to a gift shop, she announced quickly
to Donna Mae and Alex, "Bess and George and
I are going to do a little shopping. Suppose we
meet you later at Antoine's."

Without further explanation, the three girls
ducked into the shop. Donna Mae, looking impatient, followed them, but Alex remained outside. When the proprietor came forward, Bess
and George engaged him in conversation about a
flowered plate. Nancy pretended to examine a
miniature vase on a table near the window while
watching to see if the suspect passed.

To her complete astonishment, the man
stopped and spoke to Alex. It was nearly a full

minute before he moved on. Nancy signaled to Bess, who said to the proprietor:

"Thank you very much. I'll think it over."

Quickly Nancy left the shop, followed by the other girls. The suspect was not far ahead of them. Nancy started off at a brisk pace to speak to him and perhaps find a policeman.

"What's the hurry?" Alex asked, catching up to and taking her arm.

"I want to talk to someone," Nancy replied hastily. "By the way, what did the man who stopped to speak to you want?"

"That fellow! Why, he—uh—wanted to paint your picture."

"What did you say to him?" Nancy asked.

Alex laughed. "I told him there wasn't a ghost of a chance of painting you."

Nancy gazed straight at Alex to determine if he was telling the truth or teasing her. But there was only an amused look in his eyes which gave her no clue.

"I'd like to speak to the man myself, anyhow," Nancy declared and hurried on.

Alex and the other girls quickly followed, but by this time the suspect was out of sight. Nancy was annoyed at herself for letting him get away. "I'm sure he just pretended to be an artist!" she said to herself.

Alex led the way to Antoine's restaurant. Here the group walked through several crowded rooms

"I'm sure that he is the man who stole my car!"

before being shown a table. Nancy and the cousins observed with interest the walls that were covered with autographed photographs of famous persons.

"Now, Alex," Donna Mae said gaily, "let's have some of those scrumptious dishes you and I adore."

As her fiancé nodded and beckoned to a waiter, Nancy said, "Please order something special for me." She rose from the table. "And please excuse me a few minutes. I have to make a phone call."

Closing herself into a nearby booth, she got in touch with police headquarters, told her story about the stolen convertible, and the fact that she thought she had seen the suspect in town.

"We'll look into the matter at once, Miss Drew," the officer in charge promised.

"Thank you. I'm staying with Colonel Haver at Sunnymead," said Nancy and gave him the number.

The young detective hung up and started to open the door. Outside stood Alex Upgrove, staring at her intently!

CHAPTER VII

A Swamp Accident

As NANCY stepped out of the telephone booth, Alex Upgrove's eyes bored into hers. She stared back. Neither would waver, but Alex was the first to speak.

"Nancy, why didn't you tell me what was going on, so I could help you?" he chided. "I'm sure you're all wrong about that man being the car thief. But we can investigate the used-car lots in the city and see if we can find your convertible."

"Thank you, Alex, but I'll leave that to the police," Nancy replied. She was angry that Alex had followed her and deliberately listened to her conversation.

"Well, have it your own way," he said, escorting her back to the table. "But I wish you wouldn't be so mysterious. I could be a big help to you, really I could."

"No doubt," Nancy said in an offhanded way.

The young people thoroughly enjoyed their luncheon in the famous restaurant which had been operating in this same building since 1868. The lunch included the famous oysters Rockefeller, served in the half shell on hot salt, and garnished with a secret garlic sauce. Then came "chicken in the bag." The waiter tore off the paper covering, revealing a succulent rice-stuffed bird. Dessert was pecan pie.

As they left Antoine's, Bess declared she could not eat another morsel until the next day!

"Well, that's fine," said Donna Mae, laughing, "because I want to put on a rehearsal of the play and we won't have to take time out for dinner."

The visitors reluctantly acquiesced. But each was thinking that she could not become too excited about appearing in the fairy costumes. Nancy writhed inwardly at the thought of further delay in starting her investigation of the showboat mystery.

When they reached home, Donna Mae announced to her parents that rehearsal in full costumes would take place in half an hour. Colonel Haver puckered his lips and frowned.

"I was going golfing," he said.

His wife smiled. "Time is getting short, dear. Maybe we'd better have the rehearsal."

As George, a few minutes later, was zippering herself into the winged fairy costume, she suddenly burst into laughter. "If you girls think these wings will hold me up, I believe I'll fly away and escape this rehearsal."

Bess giggled. "You'd better not, or you may have Donna Mae or Alex flying after you."

When the three guests appeared on the first floor, they found the others already assembled. Colonel and Mrs. Haver looked very regal in their king and queen costumes. Donna Mae and Alex, attractive in the prince and princess garments of a bygone era, smiled graciously.

"Oh, you look adorable!" Donna Mae exclaimed, but her mother gasped. "Why, I thought the three girls were going to be ladies in waiting."

"Want to see how a winged fairy acts?" George asked impishly.

Instantly she bent double and began to do a dance step that resembled that of an Indian ceremonial. Then Bess began to chant a song in the manner of a three-year-old reciting a nursery rhyme. All but Donna Mae burst into laughter.

"I'm afraid," said Colonel Haver, "that these fairy costumes are not appropriate, Donna Mae."

"Then what are we going to do?" cried his daughter, who was on the verge of tears.

Her mother said she thought something more regal would be suitable. She herself would select new costumes for the girls.

Nancy sighed. "I had hoped to wear my mother's beautiful shawl and fan to the ball. The suitcase they were packed in was stolen, you know."

"That was most unfortunate," said Mrs. Haver. "But I'll plan your costume so that you can wear the shawl and fan that evening if you should get them back in time."

Nancy flashed her a smile. "Thank you, Mrs. Haver."

After the three fairies had unsnapped their wings and laid them on the sofa, the rehearsal began. Earlier Pappy Cole had brought in several boxes to form a platform on which the actors could perform.

"When we're acting on the showboat, we'll have a real stage," said Mrs. Haver.

"I wouldn't count on that too much, my dear," Colonel Haver remarked, "unless Nancy Drew solves the mystery."

Any reply Nancy might have made was interrupted by Bess who at that moment made a misstep on top of one of the boxes. As she fell backward onto the floor, everyone rushed forward to help her.

"Are you hurt, Bess?" Nancy asked solicitously.

"Oh, my arm!" Bess exclaimed, tears coming to her eyes. "I guess I wrenched it!"

Mrs. Haver insisted that Bess go upstairs and lie down. Nancy offered to massage the arm and George said she would get cold compresses.

"But what's going to happen to the rehearsal?" Donna Mae wailed.

"We'll have to postpone it," her mother replied.

Donna Mae continued to complain peevishly that everything would be ruined, and had her friends and family forgotten that her engagement was to be announced the night of the ball?

"Everything just *must* go smoothly!" she exclaimed.

Nancy and her friends were disgusted with the girl's attitude. Ignoring her, they climbed the stairs to George and Bess's bedroom.

"What's the matter with that cousin of ours?" George burst out.

"Oh, don't pick on her, George," said Bess. "I think Donna Mae is nervous and irritable because her conscience bothers her."

"You mean about Charles Bartolome?" Nancy asked.

"Yes."

Bess decided to spend the remainder of the afternoon and evening in her room. Nancy and George had supper with the family on the terrace. Shortly afterward, Nancy announced she was going to her room and planned to retire early.

"I've had a lovely day. Thank you so much. Good night, everyone."

As Nancy walked into the house, Alex hurried

after her. "Wait a minute, Nancy. Don't leave yet," he pleaded. "I want to talk to you. Won't you please tell me what your plans are for solving the mystery?"

"Truthfully, I haven't any," said Nancy.

As she started to walk on, Alex took her hand. "If you have no plans, may I suggest some?"

Nancy was annoyed, but she did not want to be rude. "What kind of plans?" she asked.

"Well, first of all, I think you ought to see the showboat. What say you and I get up early tomorrow morning and take a canoe out there together?"

"How early?" Nancy asked, parrying for time to think up an excuse not to accept the invitation.

"Oh, before the others are up," Alex said with a sly smile. "We'll get back for breakfast."

By this time Nancy had an answer. "Alex, I understand the bayou is very dangerous. Neither of us is familiar with it. Sorry, but I'm afraid I can't go with you."

With that, she went up the steps two at a time and hurried to her room, closing the door.

"What a pest he is!" Nancy said to herself. Then she smiled. "One thing I can do without is his company to the showboat."

Nancy sat down in a chair by the window, lost in thought. Suddenly she arose. "I'll find out right now about a guide to take me through the bayou."

The young detective decided that Mammy Matilda and Pappy Cole might know a trustworthy guide.

Nancy peered into the hall to be sure Alex was not in sight, then she hurried to a back stairway leading to the kitchen and went down. Mammy Matilda and Pappy Cole were just finishing their supper.

"That was a delicious meal," Nancy said, sitting down on a high stool. "I've never eaten anything that tasted better than that Creole rice."

The elderly couple smiled and thanked her. Then Nancy changed the subject. "I'd like to visit the old showboat. Could you recommend a good guide?"

The two servants looked frightened, and Mammy Matilda said, "Miss Nancy, you mustn't go near that there showboat."

"Why not?" the young sleuth asked. "I'm hoping to solve the mystery in connection with it."

Pappy Cole frowned. "I guess you haven't heard that there's a ghost on board. It's a haunted showboat."

"What does the ghost do?" Nancy asked.

"Oh, all kinds of things, Miss Nancy," Mammy Matilda replied. "Every time a workman goes there an' tries to fix the boat up, that there ghost comes along an' ruins all that he's done."

"Hm," said Nancy, thinking that such destruction sounded more like the work of a human being than a ghost!

"To tell you the truth," Mammy Matilda went on, "I think our folks here are makin' a big mistake tryin' to move that there boat."

"Why do you think so?" Nancy asked her.

The old couple looked questioningly at each other. Then finally Pappy Cole said, his voice rising excitedly, "The *River Princess* was sent into the bayou by a great flood. It's Providence that did it. Providence. We got no right to change things. Mammy an' I think that boat should rest there in peace."

Nancy was amazed at this point of view. Instantly she wondered if there were others in the neighborhood who felt the same as Mammy Matilda and Pappy Cole. If so, they might be responsible for what was happening!

"Well, whether the old boat is moved or not," Nancy said, "I'd love to look at it."

"Well, if you insist, Miss Nancy," said Pappy Cole, "I think there's no better man than Uncle Rufus. He knows that there bayou like the alligators do an' he's as wise as the old owls in it, too."

Nancy asked Pappy Cole if he would arrange for Uncle Rufus to come to Sunnymead so that she might talk to him.

"I'll have him here directly after breakfast," Pappy Cole promised. "Just come to the kitchen, Miss Nancy."

Delighted, she thanked the couple for the information and went back upstairs. Nancy stopped at Bess and George's room to tell them about her plan and ask them to go along. George at once accepted. Bess said she would go if her arm felt better in the morning.

By breakfast time Bess insisted that while her elbow was still sore, it did not bother her very much and she would like to see the old showboat.

At nine o'clock they went to the kitchen. A white-haired Negro immediately stood up. He was tall and slender, and his face had the look of a trustworthy, helpful person.

"This is Uncle Rufus," Mammy Matilda introduced him. "Uncle Rufus, these here girls are the ones who want to go to that showboat. Miss Drew, Miss Fayne, and Miss Marvin."

The elderly man made a low bow and said he would be very happy to take them.

"I got my ka-noo outside," he said. "When you all is ready, Uncle Rufus will paddle you up the stream."

As Nancy and George started upstairs to change their shoes, Bess walked out to the porch where the Havers were talking. Alex had gone out, they said. When Bess told them of the girls' plan, the Colonel said:

"Fine. Perhaps you'll find some clues to help solve our mystery."

"But do be careful," Mrs. Haver cautioned.

When Nancy, Bess, and George met Uncle Rufus at the rear of the garden, they looked at the canoe in amazement. It was a handmade dugout, very old and fragile looking.

"Are you sure it's safe for all of us to go?" Bess asked nervously.

Uncle Rufus smiled. "This here ka-noo has taken me an' my nieces and nephews miles an' miles," he said proudly. "Don't you all worry about it."

The girls stepped in and the old man started paddling. Soon the house vanished from sight. For some time there was no conversation as the girls tried to accustom themselves to the eerie stillness. The dismal atmosphere of the swamp and its rank odor disturbed Bess.

Uncle Rufus, seeing her holding a handkerchief to her nose, remarked, "Pretty soon you all won't mind this stench. Right hereabouts it's scarce in moss. Deeper in the swamp there's plenty of it. You know, moss is one o' God's gifts to the swamp. It purifies the air."

Farther on, the girls noticed quantities of moss growing on stumps and stones. The air did seem purer!

The sight-seers also noticed that on both sides of the stream, among the trees, was thick coarse grass.

"That's crawfish grass," Uncle Rufus told them. He explained that the natives let down net baskets on the end of a pole among the blades of grass.

"They puts in fish bait," he said, "an' in no time they gets themselves a basket full o' crawfish."

For some distance the cleared stream through the swamp was about thirty feet wide, then it suddenly narrowed. Uncle Rufus explained that this was as far as Colonel Haver had cleared it out.

As they entered the narrow part, Uncle Rufus pulled in his paddle and let the boat glide. "Want ol' Rufus to tell you 'bout the time—"

At that instant the canoe hit an underwater obstruction head on. The craft shuddered violently, then overturned, throwing its passengers into the murky water!

CHAPTER VIII

The Voodoo Preacher

UNCLE RUFUS and the girls came to the surface, shaking the mucky water from their faces. The four of them waded to the overturned dugout.

"There's a big hole in it!" George exclaimed.

Uncle Rufus shook his head in dismay, then with the girls began to look for the cause of the accident.

Suddenly Nancy cried out, "There's a barricade here!"

She had dived under the water. In its murkiness she had spotted a stout net of vines which had been strung across the narrow part of the stream and tied to trees on each side. The impact of the dugout had torn it apart.

"Hm!" said Uncle Rufus. "But that sure wasn't what put a hole in my ka-noo."

He went down under the water himself and felt around. A moment later he surfaced. He told the girls that several sharp-pointed stones had been used to weight down the vine net. These had pierced his craft.

"Someone did this on purpose to keep us from going any farther!" George declared.

Uncle Rufus looked startled. "You mean you all got some enemies around here?"

"It looks like it," Nancy agreed. "But, Uncle Rufus, maybe you know of some other reason why the vine might have been put here."

The old man shook his head. "Nobody in this here bayou has got anything against Uncle Rufus." He changed the subject abruptly. "Well, I've got to go an' get another boat. You ladies climb some trees, else some hungry ole alligator may bother you."

Bess gave a little squeal and instantly started wading toward a swamp oak.

"Where are you going to find a boat?" Nancy asked Uncle Rufus.

The old man said a friend would lend him one. He knew a short cut to the man's cabin. With a smile Uncle Rufus added that he was used to sloshing through the swamp on foot. "I won't be gone more'n half an hour," he said.

"Half an hour?" Bess wailed. "You mean I have to stay up in this tree all that time?"

"I'se afraid you do," Uncle Rufus replied.

As he was about to start off, Nancy suddenly said, "Listen! I think I hear a boat coming!"

They all remained quiet and presently a canoeist turned a bend just ahead in the narrow part of the stream.

"Alex!" Nancy exclaimed.

The young man looked up. Seeing the girls and Uncle Rufus, he called out, "What in the world is going on?"

Quickly Nancy explained. As Alex came closer he said, "A mat of vines, you say? That's strange. Apparently it wasn't here half an hour ago when I went up the stream."

"Did you see anyone else around?" Nancy asked him.

"No, I didn't," Alex answered. Then he added, "Well, all of you climb aboard and I'll take you home. I suppose you were on your way to see the showboat?"

Nancy confessed that they were. She expressed amazement that Alex had dared paddle up to the *River Princess* alone.

The young man laughed. "Oh, I'm not afraid of ghosts," he said. "These stories about that showboat being haunted are a lot of nonsense. But just the same, I'm convinced it would be foolhardy to try clearing out the rest of the stream and moving the showboat to the Havers' estate before Mardi Gras time. In fact, I think it would be silly to move the *River Princess* at any time. She isn't worth it."

"You mean the boat's in bad shape?" Bess asked.

"She sure is. Practically rotting away."

There was no further conversation on the subject until they neared the dock at Sunnymead. Then Alex remarked, "I'm going to advise Colonel Haver to call off all work and investigation. Nancy, I hope you'll back me up. Then you won't have to bother with any mystery and all of us can have a good time together."

Nancy did not reply. Instead, as the group stepped out of the canoe, she suggested to Uncle Rufus that he come inside the house. "You can bathe and borrow some clothes from Pappy Cole."

Uncle Rufus laughed. "Thank you kindly, miss, but I'se used to the swamp mud. I got a little bathin' pond of my own up to the cabin. I'll just amble along through the water till I git home."

He had gone only fifty feet when a new idea occurred to Nancy. Running along the shore, she caught up to him. In a low voice she said, "I'd still like to visit the showboat. Would it be possible for you to take the other girls and me some time today?"

"Why, yes, miss," Uncle Rufus answered. "Could you all come to my cabin when you git fixed up? I'll be ready an' I'll borrow that ka-noo I was tellin' you about."

Nancy asked directions and was told how to reach the cabin by car. "We'll be there in an hour," she said.

When Nancy returned to the rest of her group, Alex adroitly tried to find out about her conversation with Uncle Rufus. But the young detective side-stepped his questions.

"What's next on the program?" Alex inquired, as he and the girls walked toward the Haver mansion.

"A bath and a shampoo!" George announced firmly.

When the girls reached their adjoining bedrooms, Nancy whispered her plan about starting again for the showboat. Bess said that she would be glad to go but wondered how they could keep Alex from accompanying them or finding out where they were going.

"This time we're not going to tell anybody where we're going," Nancy said. "You remember Colonel Haver telling me I'd have free rein in solving this mystery and wouldn't have to report to anybody. Let's keep this trip a secret."

"Why the secrecy, Nancy?" Bess asked. "Surely you don't suspect anyone in this house of being mixed up in the mystery, do you?"

"I didn't mean that," Nancy answered. "If our plan becomes known, we may be interrupted again to go sight-seeing."

George chuckled. "Also, Bess, you don't have to be suspicious of people like Alex just because you don't like them. I suppose he means well, but I can't stand that man and I know Nancy can't."

"Well, I can't either," admitted Bess. "But, Nancy, surely you don't think *he* put that barrier rope across the river to keep us from seeing the showboat, do you?"

"No. But he's not very consistent. First, he wanted to join forces with me and solve the mystery—undoubtedly to make a hit with his future father-in-law. Now he says he's going to advise him to drop the whole proposition and even wants me to back him up!"

George laughed. "Talk about women changing their minds!"

The girls were ready in half an hour and went downstairs. Donna Mae and Alex were playing tennis on a court near the house. Colonel and Mrs. Haver, Nancy learned from Mammy Matilda, had gone to town.

Nancy and her friends left the mansion by a side door and walked to their car. Taking the service road, Nancy avoided the tennis court and drove off. Following Uncle Rufus's directions, she turned from the main road onto a bayou lane.

In a little while she came to a modest brown wooden shack in a grove of cypress trees. The girls got out and walked toward the building.

"Wait!" Bess cried out. "This can't be the right house. Do you hear what I do?"

From the cabin came the sounds of doleful chanting and the rise and fall of a wailing voice, evidently praying.

"Sounds like a voodoo session," George observed.

The girls stood still and listened. Singsong mutterings followed the chanting.

A moment later a small boy came from the cabin and ran toward the girls. "What you all want?" he asked.

"Is this Uncle Rufus's home?" Nancy inquired.

"Yassum, it is," the boy replied. "But you cain't see him now."

"But we have an appointment with him," said Nancy.

"Uncle Rufus had a 'mergency case," the boy said.

"Emergency case?" George asked. "Is Uncle Rufus a doctor?"

"Yassum," said the little boy. As he ran off, he called back, "Uncle Rufus is a voodoo doctor!"

The girls were amazed.

"I don't want Uncle Rufus casting any spells on me!" Bess said firmly.

Nancy was thoughtful. Finally she asked, "Do you suppose Uncle Rufus could head a group of voodoo believers who hold secret meetings on the showboat?"

George said it was very likely. "And perhaps

they're deliberately haunting it so the boat won't be moved!" she suggested.

"We'll try to find out. But we mustn't make Uncle Rufus suspicious," she warned, and her friends nodded.

At that moment Uncle Rufus's "patient," an elderly colored woman, came from the cabin. She was singing a hymn. As she passed the girls she smiled at them happily but did not speak.

After the woman was out of hearing distance, Bess remarked, "She acts as if she were in a trance!"

"She sure does," said George.

Just then Uncle Rufus appeared. As if reading the girls' thoughts, he explained that when the woman had come to visit him she had been limping. A radiant expression spread over the old man's face when he added, "Now through prayer she's cured. We sang an' we prayed together."

In unison the girls said, "We're glad," but made no other reference to the woman or the subject of voodooism.

For several seconds Uncle Rufus stood looking after his "patient," then he turned to the girls, "I'se ready to take the trip now."

CHAPTER IX

The River Princess

THE CANOE proceeded along the bayou stream in leisurely fashion. Uncle Rufus paddled evenly but slowly. Now and then he would stop along the edge to point out an herb.

"Are some of them spices?" Nancy asked.

Uncle Rufus said a few were, but most of the swamp herbs were used for medicinal purposes.

Now that the old man had started talking about the bayou, he went on and on, telling about its wild life. "Take spiders," he said. "They represents the devil on this earth. They pi-son folks, an' snakes do, too. You got to be mighty careful of 'em."

Uncle Rufus said that on the other hand the turtle represented great patience. "Just like God's patience with man," he added, smiling. "And a turtle knows enough not to stick its neck out an' get into other folks' business."

As the girls chuckled, Uncle Rufus suddenly called their attention to a screeching sound. "Know what that is?"

"Oh, it's a birdcall, isn't it?" George asked.

Uncle Rufus nodded. "Do you know what kind?"

"A wild duck?" Nancy guessed.

"No," Uncle Rufus replied, "but somebody's sure 'nuff tryin' to imitate one."

"Is it being used as a signal?" Nancy asked.

"Mebbe so," Uncle Rufus answered. "But it's an awful bad imitation. Nobody who knows the bayou would be fooled by that."

Just then from the opposite direction came another call, exactly the same as the first. The girls exchanged meaningful glances. Who *was* imitating a wild duck's cry? Suddenly Uncle Rufus chuckled and said that a couple of city boys must be playing a game in the bayou.

Nancy and her friends, although they did not say so aloud, did not come to the same conclusion. It was possible that persons were signaling with some sinister purpose—perhaps to set another trap for the girls!

Meanwhile, the canoe had already entered the narrow part of the stream. Fifteen minutes later Uncle Rufus sang out:

"The *River Princess* is just ahead!"

He paddled around a bend and the girls found themselves facing a small pond. At the far side of it, against a backdrop of moss-covered oaks, lay the old showboat.

It was about a hundred feet long, twenty-five feet wide, and had two decks. The craft had listed slightly and its lookout tower had been damaged by a falling tree.

Uncle Rufus chuckled. "I—I guess the *River Princess* was plenty proud in her day. Hundreds of gentlefolks used to come to see the shows."

Bess gave a great, audible sigh. "I don't blame Colonel Haver for wanting to restore the *River Princess*. She's the most romantic thing I've seen in a long time."

"And one of the worst wrecks," George retorted.

Nancy smiled. "I agree, partly, with both of you. But really I don't think this showboat is beyond repair. Let's go aboard and look for ourselves."

At that moment hammering started on the craft. Bess involuntarily gave a shudder and Uncle Rufus looked startled.

Nancy grinned and said quickly, "Don't worry. Ghosts rarely work in the daytime." In a louder voice she called, "Anybody home?"

A moment later a tall young man appeared on the lower deck and walked toward the railing. He was fine-featured and had reddish hair.

"That must be Charles Bartolome," Bess said in a low voice. "I've seen his picture."

"That's Mr. Bartolome all right," Uncle Rufus spoke up.

The young man, after his first look of surprise at seeing callers, smiled at the group in the canoe. "Hi!" he called.

Introductions were quickly exchanged. Under her breath, Bess murmured, "How in the world could Donna Mae ever have switched from him to Alex Upgrove?" Nancy and George shared the same feeling but made no comment.

Nancy told Charles Bartolome why she and her friends had come to the showboat and how she hoped to clear up the mystery.

"We want to have the *River Princess* brought to Sunnymead, so that the ball the Havers are planning will be a big success."

"I, too, would like to see the mystery solved," said Charles. He did not mention the ball. "Good luck to you all."

"We'll probably need your help," Nancy told him. "As a start, would you mind showing us around the *River Princess*?"

"I'd be delighted to," he replied. "I've become very fond of the old gal. But as soon as my job of restoring the showboat is completed, I'm leaving for New York. I'm going to live there permanently and continue my work as an architect."

The girls were sure they knew the reason for the move. With Donna Mae married to Alex, he would no longer want to live in the New Orleans neighborhood.

Uncle Rufus waited in the canoe while the girls climbed a ladder and went aboard. Charles led them inside to the auditorium. Fastened to the sloping floor were many rows of old-fashioned, cushioned opera chairs. A balcony, ornate in design, ran around three sides of the room, and on the fourth side was a stage. A tattered red-and-gold curtain hung down at the front of it.

Charles remarked cheerfully, "A couple of coats of paint will do wonders for the *River Princess*. Actually the old boat is not in such bad shape. It's just—" The young man paused.

His listeners waited for him to go on. Finally he said, "It's just that we can't find anybody willing to work on her or move her. And the men who were clearing out this part of the stream won't continue."

"Is it because they were frightened by something which happened on the boat?"

"Oh, there have been all sorts of rumors," Charles replied. "One was that the calliope on board actually played. That would be impossible, of course. The old organ has been out of commission for years."

Charles went on to say that he himself had done some work in starting the restoration of the *River Princess,* but that what he had rebuilt was mysteriously hacked during the night.

"That's a shame," said Nancy.

"But I'm not discouraged," Charles replied. "I'll keep at it."

Nancy smiled, then said, "Bess and George and I have wondered if people in the area who practice voodoo may be using this place for their meetings. Do you think that's possible?"

Charles Bartolome considered this idea for several seconds, then he said, "It's possible. But why would they destroy my work?"

Nancy suggested that it might be to frighten him away. "In any case, these people would not want the showboat moved to a place where they could no longer use it, and might be using various means to discourage Colonel Haver."

The young man smiled. "Well, Nancy, it's your mystery. Come, I'll show you the rest of the boat."

The ticket office and captain's suite were at the bow of the boat, while at the stern, back of the stage, were dressing rooms and living quarters.

"These bedrooms were for married couples," the young architect explained. "The unmarried men stayed on the steam towboat that pushed the *River Princess* from place to place. The kitchen and dining room were on the towboat also."

As the tour ended on the lower deck, near the ladder, Nancy suddenly leaned over to pick up something from a crack between the boards.

"I think I have my first clue!" she cried out.

CHAPTER X

A Curious Alligator

As NANCY's friends on the showboat watched, she picked up a glittering object from a crack between the deck boards. It was a large, gold ornamental hairpin, old-fashioned in design. Tiny diamonds and emeralds sparkled from the fan-shaped end, which was about two inches wide.

"The gold is still shiny," Nancy observed, scrutinizing the pin, "so this probably hasn't been here very long."

Bess and George, too, were intrigued. "You mean the pin might have been dropped here recently by its owner?" asked George.

As Nancy nodded, the girls noticed a strange expression come over Charles Bartolome's face. He had been staring intently for several minutes at the hairpin.

"Do you know who the owner is?" George asked him.

"Possibly," the young man replied after a long moment of silence. "A few months ago Mrs. Haver showed me her collection of old jewelry. There was a hairpin exactly like this one among the pieces."

The girls were stunned by this information. It was incredible, they thought, that Mrs. Haver would have worn the ornament to the showboat. Then who had?

"Have you any theory as to how the pin got here?" Nancy asked Charles.

"Perhaps someone stole it from Mrs. Haver and dropped it accidentally," he offered.

Bess was inclined to think that the pin might not have been dropped accidentally. "Perhaps someone planted it here on purpose!"

"But why?" George asked.

Since no one could even attempt to solve the riddle at the moment, the subject was dropped. Nancy pocketed the hairpin with the thought of questioning Mrs. Haver about it later. The young detective now asked Charles if he had heard any birdcalls earlier.

"You mean the wild ducks that were answering each other?"

"Yes, only according to Uncle Rufus they weren't genuine calls. He suggested that some boys were playing a game. But we girls thought that perhaps someone might be spying on the showboat. A confederate some distance away could have been using the call to warn someone that we were approaching."

Charles frowned. "That could be true. If so, I don't like it at all. I must admit my work kept me so busy that I didn't notice anyone around."

Next, Nancy told the young architect about the vine barrier in the stream.

"This *is* serious," he said. "I'll ask Uncle Rufus to search the swamp."

He called down softly to Uncle Rufus, requesting him to hunt for any persons who might be watching the group on the boat. As the old man nodded and paddled off, Nancy suggested that the rest of them make certain no one was hiding on the boat itself.

The searchers separated, with Charles offering to go down into the hold of the vessel to find out if anyone were there. Nancy took the dressing rooms and upper deck, Bess the auditorium, and George the stage.

A thorough search was made. Doors to rooms and closets creaked on their hinges as they were opened, but all were empty except for spider webs.

Bess, after looking in the theater, wandered along one of the nearby corridors. With a start, she suddenly saw a reflection in a full-length mirror on the wall ahead of her. The frame was tarnished with age and the figure looked wavery.

"Oh!" she cried with a little shiver. Then,

realizing the reflection was her own, she ran out on deck.

"This is positively the spookiest place I've ever been in!" she said to Nancy, who had just come down from investigating the lookout and second deck.

Soon George joined them, then Charles. All reported there was no evidence that anyone besides themselves was aboard.

A few moments later Uncle Rufus returned. He reported that there was no one within a hundred yards of the *River Princess*. "I sure did look sharp every which way," the elderly man assured them. Then he added that he must leave soon.

"We'll be ready in a few minutes," Nancy told him. She turned to Charles and asked him if he had ever been on the showboat after dark.

"No, I haven't," he said. "In fact, I've never even been in the bayou after sundown." Then, reading Nancy's thoughts, he asked, "Would you girls like to visit the *River Princess* some evening with me?"

"Oh, we'd love to," Nancy replied.

Charles Bartolome offered to bring them to the showboat the following evening. Bess did not look enthusiastic, but managed to smile feebly. George declared it would be an interesting adventure. "Maybe after dark we'll be able to scare up those showboat spooks," she said.

At this, Bess's faint smile faded completely.

She threw a withering glance at her cousin and said, "Don't sound so happy about it. If we do come across any ghosts, you can catch them all, George Fayne!"

Nancy, George, and Charles chuckled, then Nancy said:

"It will be a wonderful trip. And, Charles, if you don't mind, I'd like to keep it a secret."

He grinned, gave the girls a wink, and said, "I understand. And I'm very flattered that you're going to permit me to help you solve the mystery."

"It may be a long pull," Nancy warned him.

Charles said he realized that. "But if it isn't solved by Mardi Gras time, I guess there won't be much use."

After Nancy and her friends had climbed down the ladder and were seated in the canoe, he called to them, "How about you girls coming to my home to dinner tomorrow evening before we go? I know Mother would like very much to meet you. Dad would too, but he's away for a few days."

"That's very kind," said Nancy. "I'd love to come."

"I'd be thrilled," Bess spoke up, and George added her thanks.

"Then Mother will be calling you," Charles promised.

The girls waved good-by as Uncle Rufus

"Nancy! Watch out!" Bess screamed

started paddling down the stream. On the return trip he entertained them with stories of Negro life in Africa centuries ago.

"It was my ancestors that invented the first long-distance com-mun-i-cation," he said proudly. "We made drums that could carry sounds for miles an' miles. The folks in one place sent signals an' messages by beatin' on the drums with their hands. Then the next village would pick it up an' send the signal on to another place far away. That's how they got all the members of a tribe together for special meetin's an' for fightin' wars."

"Very ingenious," George remarked.

Not once did Uncle Rufus refer to voodooism or to the fact that he himself was a voodoo doctor or preacher.

Just before the canoe reached the area in the stream where it joined the cleared section, the craft floated over a large pad of white lilies.

"Aren't they pretty?" Bess asked.

Nancy nodded and decided to pick a few of the flowers to take to Mrs. Haver. In pulling the first one, she felt the whole root coming away. She yanked at it hard and in a moment felt the clump pull loose.

The same instant, Bess, who was watching her chum, screamed. She had seen the snout of an alligator rising from beneath the leaves. The reptile's jaws were aiming for Nancy's hand!

"Look out!" Bess yelled.

CHAPTER XI

A Puzzling Attitude

BESS's cry alerted Nancy. Just in time she saw the reptile and quickly pulled in her hand, still holding the lily plant.

"Oh!" Bess gave a huge sigh of relief.

But the next moment her fright returned. Nancy and George, too, were alarmed. The alligator, as if annoyed because he had been disturbed, turned, flipping his tail. It whacked the canoe so hard that the little craft almost overturned.

Uncle Rufus stood up and hit the alligator's head with his paddle. The elderly man succeeded in stunning the alligator by hitting the vulnerable aperture behind the reptile's ear. Then Uncle Rufus sat down and began to paddle furiously downstream.

"Whew!" George burst out. "I never want to get that close to such a beast again!"

"Nor I," said Bess with a shudder. "Oh, you're so brave, Uncle Rufus!"

The old Negro's face broke into a broad grin. "When you lives with 'gators all your life, you don't fool around with 'em!" he said.

When they reached the old man's cabin, the girls thanked him for his help, then returned to Sunnymead in Nancy's car. There, tea was being served on the patio and Mrs. Haver invited the girls to join the group.

"My, but you all look mysterious," Donna Mae remarked. "Let me guess—you've been in the bayou."

When Bess confessed that they had been, Alex added, "And I'd like to bet you've been to the showboat."

"You're right," Nancy admitted. Before Alex could pursue the subject, she added, "The most exciting part of our trip was meeting an alligator."

"Oh, how positively horrid!" Donna Mae exclaimed.

The story was told in detail and Nancy hoped that no further reference would be made to the showboat. But Alex had not forgotten it.

"Well," he spoke up, "now that you've seen the *River Princess,* I'm sure you'll agree with me that it's a hopeless mess. There's no point in trying to move the boat from the bayou. It would be much too expensive."

"But, Alex dear, what are we going to do about a place to hold the ball?" Donna Mae asked.

"Don't you worry, honey," Alex said reassuringly. "I have a splendid idea. We can turn this house into a showboat!"

For a moment the Havers and their daughter were stunned by the suggestion. But presently, as Alex explained how all the furniture could be moved from the living room and a stage erected at one end, they became interested.

"If we can't have the real thing," remarked the Colonel, "I suppose we'd better start making plans immediately to decorate this place."

The girls from River Heights, however, were extremely disappointed at this turn of events and took no part in the planning. They thought Alex's suggestion a poor substitute for the Colonel's original idea—and Nancy herself did not want to give up an unsolved mystery.

Presently Alex left the group to look over the living room and decide how he would dismantle it. Mrs. Haver mentioned to her visitors that the family had been invited to a neighbor's home to a dinner party the following evening. "Would you girls like to accompany us? You're invited," she said.

"We'd love to, but the three of us have already made another engagement," Nancy told her hostess.

"Why, how nice! But I didn't realize you knew anyone down here," said Mrs. Haver, and Donna Mae asked, "Where are you going?"

Nancy told them about having met Charles

Bartolome, and the invitation to his home to dinner. Mrs. Haver, at first surprised, looked embarrassed when Donna Mae suddenly burst into tears and fled from the room. Excusing herself, the woman hurried after her daughter.

"How odd," said George. "What ails Donna Mae, anyhow!"

"Maybe we shouldn't have said anything about Charles to her," Nancy suggested.

"Do you think we ought to turn down the invitation?" Bess asked. "It seems to have upset Donna Mae terribly and we *are* guests here."

"Of course we shouldn't give it up," her cousin said determinedly. "This is a good opportunity for us to find out more about the mystery of the showboat."

As the girls quietly discussed the situation, Mrs. Haver returned and requested Nancy and her friends not to go to the Bartolomes.

"Donna Mae is in hysterics," she said. "Nancy, suppose you go upstairs and tell her you've changed your mind."

The young sleuth went to Donna Mae's bedroom. Expecting to find the girl in tears, Nancy was surprised to see the bride-to-be seated at her dressing table, putting on make-up.

"Donna Mae," Nancy began, "I'm sorry that I—"

"Oh, don't be sorry about anything," Donna Mae said airily, admiring her left profile in the mirror. "Go to the Bartolomes if you wish. It means nothing to me."

Nancy was both perplexed and amused by the girl's seeming change of heart. But she was convinced that Donna Mae was putting on an act and that she was actually in love with Charles —only too proud to admit it.

"You don't mind if we accept?" Nancy asked.

"Certainly not," Donna Mae replied. "And please tell Mother for me."

Nancy hurried downstairs. She met Mrs. Haver in the hall and gave her Donna Mae's message. The hostess forced a laugh and said, "Well, I'm glad that's straightened out."

Just then, the telephone rang and she went to answer it. A few moments later Mrs. Haver came out to the patio where Nancy had rejoined her friends. Their hostess said that Mrs. Bartolome had called to confirm the dinner invitation.

"She'll expect you girls at seven."

Later, when Nancy was alone in her own room with Bess and George, she told them of her conversation with Donna Mae and added her own thought that the girl was still in love with her ex-fiancé.

"Then let's get them together again!" Bess declared.

Nancy smiled. "But first, let's solve the mystery. I want to show Mrs. Haver the lovely old hairpin I found."

Knowing that their hostess always rested before dinner, Nancy waited until a few minutes before seven, then went to Mrs. Haver's bedroom, and tapped lightly on the door. "Come in!" the woman called.

"Oh, how pretty you look!" she said, admiring Nancy's powder-blue eyelet-embroidered dress.

"Thank you. Mrs. Haver, I have something to show you," Nancy said. She told the woman of her discovery and held up the hairpin.

"Why, how strange—how very strange!" Without another word, Mrs. Haver rushed to her bureau, opened a drawer, and took out a jewel box. She rummaged through it and a few seconds later held up a hairpin very much like the one the young detective had found.

"For a moment I thought the one you had *was* mine, Nancy," she said. "These two are almost identical. I wonder who could have dropped the other one."

"So do I," Nancy confided.

For the next ten minutes Nancy discussed the strange affair with Mrs. Haver, but neither could come to any conclusion. Finally the two walked down the stairs to dinner.

Donna Mae had completely recovered her composure. Her conversation was scintillating and the Northern girls were amazed that her attitude had changed so quickly and so completely.

Toward the end of the meal, Donna Mae smiled

gaily and announced, "I have a wonderful surprise for you girls. Alex has invited all of us to New Orleans for a gala time tomorrow."

Nancy, although she really would have preferred continuing her sleuthing, politely expressed her appreciation. She thought it advisable not to antagonize Donna Mae further. Bess said she was eager to see more of the city and eat at another famous restaurant.

George, for her part, was suspicious of Donna Mae's motives. Later, as the girls were getting ready for bed, she said, "Nancy, we'd better take your car. This trip to town may be a trick to keep us there so late that we won't be back in time to go to the Bartolomes' for dinner."

"You could be right, George," Bess agreed. "But you know I just can't figure out Donna Mae and the way she acts."

George remarked with a great yawn, "Donna Mae just isn't herself since Alex came into her life. I think it's a shame!" The girl's voice rose as she added, "She used to be such a swell person. Now she's a pain!"

"S-sh!" Nancy warned. "She may hear you."

The following morning Nancy awakened to a sunny day and the twittering chorus of birds. Going to a window, she stood there, breathing in the balmy, fragrant air and admiring the lovely gardens. Pappy Cole, a huge basket over his arm, was cutting flowers near the house.

As Nancy went into her friends' room, the aroma of broiling ham and fresh-baked corncakes wafted upstairs. "Get up, you sleepyheads," she said to Bess and George. "It's simply heavenly outside! Let's wear our skirt, blouse, and shorts sets today."

"Will do," George replied, jumping out of bed and making a beeline for the shower.

"Oh, don't rush me," Bess begged from her bed. "It's too delicious a day to hurry."

Nevertheless, the girls were dressed in half an hour and went downstairs. As soon as breakfast was over, the young people met in the driveway. Alex had the station wagon ready and hopped out to assist the passengers.

"Thank you," said Nancy, "but Bess and George and I are going in my car. We'll follow you."

A look of annoyance creased the young man's forehead. "But why?" he asked.

Bess put on an engaging smile. In a very convincing voice she said with a giggle, "You two sweetie pies ought to be alone."

To avoid any further objection, the girls hurried to Nancy's car. She followed Alex at a distance of about thirty feet all the way to New Orleans. Upon reaching the outskirts, she wondered why he did not go directly into the city. Instead, he turned and took a very circuitous route to reach the sight-seeing area.

"Nothing special here," George complained.

"Just a lot of old houses on a deserted street."

At that moment a small wad of paper fluttered from Alex's car window. Nancy, wondering whether he had dropped it by accident, decided on a sudden impulse to stop and retrieve the paper. She pulled to the curb and George hopped out to pick it up.

"This isn't anything special," George announced, climbing in and smoothing out the tiny sheet. "Just a funny drawing."

The three girls gazed at a maroon-colored rectangle with a gold stripe running through it. There was no writing on the paper.

Alex had stopped and now backed up to see what was detaining Nancy. She handed the paper to him out her window. "Did you mean to drop this?" she asked.

"Oh, that!" said Alex. "A kid cousin of mine drew it. I just found it in my pocket. I don't want it." He tossed the paper into the street and started off again.

Once more Nancy followed Alex, but as he turned a corner she suddenly stopped the car. Opening the door, she got out.

"Quick, George, take the wheel!" she ordered. "I have some sleuthing to do. Meet you at twelve o'clock at Broussard's restaurant."

Mysteriously Nancy dashed back up the street.

CHAPTER XII

A Sly Getaway

"WHAT do you think Nancy is going to do?" Bess asked her cousin, as they drove on.

"Search me!" George answered. "But you can be sure it has something to do with that wad of paper."

"You mean Nancy's figured out that the drawing on it meant something important? And Alex wasn't telling the truth when he said it had been drawn by a little cousin of his?"

"Something of the sort." George grinned. "I can just see Alex's face when we get to the parking lot. He'll be furious."

George's prediction was right. Alex and Donna Mae got out of the station wagon and walked toward the spot where George was parking. Not seeing Nancy, Alex instantly asked where she was.

"Left us to do some sleuthing," said George, as

she and Bess alighted. "She told us to meet her at Broussard's at twelve."

Alex's eyes flashed and Donna Mae looked hurt. "I don't think that's very nice of Nancy when we planned such a gay sight-seeing trip," Donna Mae remarked.

"Well, after all, Nancy was invited down here to solve a mystery," George defended her friend.

"I'm going to find her!" Alex said suddenly. He ran to the station wagon, got in, and roared out of the parking lot.

"And I'm going to follow," George said to herself. She got behind the wheel of Nancy's car and sped after the young man.

Donna Mae and Bess stared after the two cars. "Well, of all the horrid things to do!" Donna Mae cried out pettishly.

"What difference does it make?" Bess said soothingly. "You and I can have some fun shopping together."

This did not appease Donna Mae, however. She insisted upon waiting at the parking lot. But when ten minutes had gone by and the others had not returned, she finally consented to leaving.

In the meantime, Nancy had run back to the spot where Alex had thrown the drawing into the street. Instinct urged her to find out more about the piece of paper.

To Nancy's astonishment, the paper was gone!

"And there is no street cleaner or anyone else in sight," Nancy murmured to herself.

Her latest suspicion that Alex was not entirely trustworthy instantly became stronger. It seemed as if the circuitous route into town might have had a real purpose behind it. Had Alex, by prearrangement, deliberately dropped the paper for someone to pick up?

Her mind racing, Nancy wondered if the paper might have been a signal, perhaps to a person in a house nearby.

"Maybe I'm being watched myself," Nancy thought, and she was determined to find out what she could.

Standing exactly where the paper had been dropped, she studied the two facing houses on opposite sides of the street. Both were old-fashioned but well kept. Neither gave any outward indication of mysterious goings-on.

As Nancy stood reflecting what to do next, a young colored woman, with a market basket over her arm, came from one of the houses. Nancy stepped up to her and smiled.

"Would you mind answering a question?" she asked. "I'm a stranger in town—here for the Mardi Gras. This part of your city is quite unfamiliar to me and I'm looking for someone. Do you mind telling me who lives in the house where you work?"

The pretty young woman chuckled. "One of

the finest families in New Orleans lives here. And this street used to be a nice quiet one. But now it's noisy and all on account of the people from New York who live across the street."

Instantly Nancy was interested. "A family from New York, you say?"

"Not a family," the girl replied. "It's a boardinghouse run by a woman who takes tourists sent by a New York travel agency. I shouldn't gossip about our neighbors, but they're not the kind of folks we're used to around here. They're loud and commonlike."

Nancy expressed sympathy, then thanked the girl for the information.

"You're welcome," said the young woman and walked away.

"Tourists from New York," Nancy repeated to herself. "Alex is from New York."

Then another thought struck her. The car thief from the North might stay in this kind of place! Confused but eager to find out what she could, Nancy, on a hunch, opened the side gate of the property and hurried to the rear of the yard.

Several cars were parked there and Nancy went from one to another. Suddenly her heart began to beat faster. Near the side fence and backed against a hedge that separated the property from the house beside it stood a black convertible. It had black-and-red seat cushions!

Nancy excitedly opened the door to look at the carpet. Perhaps she could find out if it also was torn as hers had been!

Before she had a chance to look, the kitchen door of the house opened. A slovenly-looking woman, with unkempt hair, rushed outside and waved her fists at Nancy.

"What are you doing on my property!" she cried out. "I'll have the police after you!"

Nancy quickly closed the car door. She memorized the number of the Louisiana license plate on it and said sweetly, "I'm looking for someone who has a car just like this. Would you mind telling me who owns this one?"

The woman did not reply to Nancy's question. Instead, she gave the young sleuth a tongue-lashing about people who pried, and ordered her to leave the yard at once.

"Sorry," said Nancy. "I'll go."

As she walked toward the street, the young detective glanced from window to window for any sign of the car thief but she saw no one.

"Nancy!" a voice called from the sidewalk. Turning, Nancy was surprised to see George and Alex standing there.

The young man scowled. "What are you going to do next," he chided her.

"Get the police," Nancy replied.

"The police!" Alex replied in astonishment.

"What's up?" George wanted to know.

Nancy quickly explained about finding the car.

"We'll all go to the police station," Alex announced, adding that he would do all he could to help her.

"Suppose you and George go," Nancy proposed. "If the man who stole my car is in this house, he may try to get away. I'll stay here and watch."

Alex hesitated, obviously reluctant to accept the suggestion, but finally remarked, "I suppose you'll be all right alone," and drove off with George in the station wagon.

Nancy went to sit in her own car and wait. Her eyes did not leave the house. Presently Alex and George returned in the station wagon. Behind them was a police car with two officers. While one of them remained on the sidewalk, the other hurried to the rear of the house with Nancy and her friends.

The black car was gone!

It was clear what had happened. The convertible had been backed through the hedge and driven out the adjoining property to the street beyond. Nancy berated herself for not having prevented the escape.

"Did you notice the license number?" the officer asked.

Nancy gave it to him, but said, "If the person who drove the car away is the same one who stole it in River Heights, he'll substitute other license plates at once."

"You're no doubt right," the policeman agreed. "I'll alert headquarters immediately."

The group returned to the sidewalk and the information was relayed to headquarters. Then one of the officers went with Nancy to interview the woman in the house.

When she answered the bell, the boarding-house owner glared at Nancy. "You back?"

"We'd like to ask you a few questions," the officer said, showing his identification. "Who owns the car that was driven away through the hedge?"

"Nobody I know," the woman answered. "Tourist agency sent him here. Said his name was John Lane and he was from New York City. I don't know anything about him. Why are you asking all this?"

"This young lady here thinks the man was driving a stolen car," the officer explained. "It's a serious charge, and if you're keeping back any information about your boarders, you may find yourself in difficulty with the police."

Hearing this, the woman lost her bravado. Over and over she repeated that she knew nothing about the man. Nancy asked her if she could give them a description of Mr. Lane. When this had been done, Nancy said:

"The description fits the man who stole my convertible!"

"I'm sure Mr. Lane won't come back," the boardinghouse mistress said. "But if he does, I'll let you know."

As the policeman went down the steps with Nancy, he assured her that the police would do everything in their power to track down the thief. Nancy and George followed Alex to the parking lot and once more they pulled their automobiles into position.

Since Donna Mae and Bess had left, Alex offered to show the other girls something of the newer part of New Orleans. He pointed out Canal Street, one of the widest thoroughfares in the world. He said that originally there had been a canal in the center of it which had been used to drain off excessive rain water.

Many people were walking on the street and along the adjoining side streets. Alex explained that thousands of tourists came from all parts of the country to help celebrate the Mardi Gras.

"The parades always disband on Canal Street," he told the girls.

At twelve o'clock they went to Broussard's restaurant. Donna Mae and Bess were waiting for them and insisted upon a full explanation of where they had been.

When Donna Mae heard the story, she remarked, "What a shame! I'm sorry you had bad luck not finding out about your car, Nancy. But why bother about it? Goodness, I wouldn't want to ride in a car that had been driven by such an awful man." Then she lapsed into silence.

As the group began to eat, Bess told of buying several attractive souvenirs to take home. "Mostly pralines and pecan nougat," she confessed. "But I did get some lovely prints of New Orleans."

Donna Mae remained very quiet. What little she said seemed to be forced. But as the dessert was served, she suddenly became animated.

"I've just had the most wonderful idea," she announced. "I'm going to invite Ned Nickerson, Burt Eddleton, and Dave Evans down for the Mardi Gras!"

Nancy smiled. "That's very sweet of you, Donna Mae, and of course we'd love to see the boys. But I doubt that they could take the time away from college."

A gleam came into Donna Mae's eyes. She said meaningly, "They won't dare refuse!"

CHAPTER XIII

Mississippi Mishap

THE IMPLIED threat in Donna Mae's remark angered Nancy, Bess, and George. All of them were sure what the girl had in mind: She did not want either Alex or Charles to make any dates with Nancy and her friends. She was going to make the boys from Emerson College so jealous they would not dare refuse to come to New Orleans!

None of the three girls expressed their thoughts aloud, however. Instead, Bess said sweetly, "Oh, I'd adore to see Dave Evans!"

"There's no one I'd rather date than Burt Eddleton," George spoke up quickly.

Nancy added, "I'm sure the boys would have a wonderful time here if they can come. And I must admit that I prefer Ned to any other escort."

George grinned. "I'll tell you one thing,

Donna Mae. Burt will never consent to putting on the costume of a fairy prince for your ball!"

Her remark eased the tension and everyone laughed.

The subject was dropped when Alex announced, "Now for some more sight-seeing. I've rented a launch and we'll show you girls the river."

"That sounds alluring," Bess commented. "The Mississippi is such a romantic river."

"It's more than that," Alex told her. "It's one of the busiest."

They drove through several narrow streets until they came to the waterfront, lined with docks and ships at anchor. Donna Mae said it was one of the most important shipping points in the world.

"Millions of tons of cargo go through here every year. One thing is of particular interest. The New Orleans port is known as a foreign trade zone. This means that foreign vessels coming in here can unload and have the cargo transferred to another ship going out of the United States without payment of customs duty."

By this time, they had reached the dock where the rented launch was tied up. It was a trim craft with a small cabin. The group eagerly climbed aboard and Alex took the wheel.

Soon the launch was out in the middle of the stream. The sight-seers looked up and down the river at the great docks, where vessels of various sizes and kinds were moored.

"See that white boat over there?" Donna Mae pointed. "That's a banana boat. It's painted white so the sun will be reflected. In this way the hold where the fruit is stored remains cool."

They passed a small puffing tug which was pushing a string of cargo boats. George remarked that the little tugs must have tremendous power.

"They do," said Alex. "And of course the flowing river helps a little. It's only when the tugs go upstream that they have to work hard."

Part of the tour led past huge grain elevators. Alex remarked, "Those long conveyors you see can load eighteen thousand bushels an hour onto the ships."

"Yes," Donna said, and added, "The grain barges can hold as much as three thousand bushels!"

"I suppose," said George, "that the bananas are incoming cargo and the grain is outgoing."

"That's right," Donna Mae replied. "The grain goes to countries in many parts of the world."

The New Orleans girl now proudly said that the United States engineers had conquered the problem of floods for the city.

"It used to be perfectly frightening when the old river overflowed and the levees broke," she said. "When the Mississippi goes on a rampage now, some of the water is pumped into Lake Pontchartrain miles above here. The excess is carried through steel-reinforced concrete tunnels to a point fifteen miles below the city. You wouldn't believe it, but there are a thousand miles of pipe!"

Presently Alex turned upstream and Donna Mae said she wanted the girls to see some of the plantation homes along the upper river. Soon they left the area of traffic. Only now and then they passed a boat.

"What a divine place to live!" Bess remarked, gazing at pecan orchards framing a lovely old house.

Presently Nancy glanced at her watch. "I think we'd better turn back now," she suggested, thinking of the girls' dinner engagement at the Bartolomes. "It's getting late."

"Oh, no!" Donna Mae protested. "You haven't seen anything yet."

George laughed. "I've seen so much, I'm sure I won't be able to remember it all."

Nevertheless, Alex went on for several miles more, with Donna Mae pointing out the high concrete levees in some places and farm land running right down to the river in others. Again Nancy asked Alex to turn around.

"Okay," he agreed, making a wide sweep in the river and coming about at five hundred yards from the far shore. Suddenly the motor began to sputter and the next moment it stopped.

"Goodness, what's the matter?" Donna Mae asked.

Alex gave a great sigh. "We're out of gas!"

Nancy was angry. Why hadn't Alex checked the tank before they left? Aloud she merely said, "There must be an emergency can on board."

All the young people searched. They opened every locker, but there was no extra fuel in any of them.

"Well, this is a fine mess!" George exclaimed in disgust.

The three River Heights girls looked at one another, the same thought in all their minds. Had Alex and Donna Mae planned this on purpose to keep them from going to the Bartolome home to dinner?

"If they are guilty, I'm not going to let them get the better of me," Nancy determined silently. Aloud she cried out, "Help! Help!"

Bess and George yelled also. Alex and Donna Mae sat still, smiling amusedly. When no one appeared in answer to the girls' call, George looked at Alex and demanded:

"Well, aren't you going to do something?"

"What can I do?" the young man replied, shrugging. "We'll get back sooner or later. The stream will carry us down slowly and we'll meet someone who will give us gas."

Such a delay was not to Nancy's liking. She decided to do something at once. "I'm going for help," she announced.

Standing up, she kicked off her shoes and then unfastened the skirt of her three-piece ensemble. Before the others could object, she dived overboard, and began swimming with strong strokes for shore.

"She's crazy!" Alex exclaimed. "She may never make shore. And if she does, there's probably not a house for miles around."

Bess was almost persuaded to his viewpoint. But George said confidently, "Nancy will make it all right."

Nancy did swim the five hundred yards easily. She crawled up the low levee, then disappeared from view. The others waited anxiously.

Presently they heard the hum of a motor starting up, and from around a bend in the river came a small motorboat. In it were Nancy and a middle-aged farmer. On a seat stood a five-gallon can of gas.

With little ado, the fuel was poured into the tank of the rented craft and Alex paid the man. Nancy thanked the farmer for all his trouble and climbed back into the launch. Alex started the motor and headed for New Orleans.

"Oh, Nancy, you're wonderful!" Donna Mae said. "Simply wonderful! I'd never have had the nerve to do that."

Bess and George looked at their chum admiringly, adding their praise also. Alex, however, kept silent.

Nancy herself merely laughed. "I must be a sight," she declared. "Bess, lend me a clean handkerchief, will you?"

With it, Nancy tried to wipe the muddy water from her face, neck, and arms, but with little success. The wind soon dried her hair and clothes.

After she had put on her skirt and shoes, Nancy noticed that the launch was going very slowly. She urged Alex to speed up. He made no comment, but did give the craft more power.

As soon as they reached the dock, Nancy, Bess, and George hopped out. "Thank you so much for a grand trip," Nancy said. "Now we must hurry. If you don't mind, we'll grab a taxi back to the parking lot. Then we'll hurry on home."

By the time the girls reached Sunnymead, it was already six-thirty. Only half an hour before dinner at the Bartolomes'!

"Bess," said Nancy, "will you please call Charles's mother and explain why we'll be a little late. I'll dash right upstairs and wash the Mississippi mud out of my hair. And, George, will you get some clothes we can wear on our bayou trip tonight and hide them in the trunk of the car?"

A few minutes later Bess came to Nancy's

room. She reported that Mrs. Bartolome had graciously said she would postpone the dinner hour to eight o'clock. George said the sports clothes and shoes were in the car.

By seven-thirty the girls were ready to leave. As they walked into the hall, Donna Mae, looking very attractive in a peach-colored organdy, came from her room.

"Have a wonderful time, girls," she said. "I should warn you, though, that Mrs. Bartolome goes to bed early. You'll be back here by ten."

George flushed with anger. She said icily, "We'll be here when we get here!"

Donna Mae looked as if she had been stung. To ease the tension, Nancy said quickly, "Do have a nice time at your dinner party."

The three girls hurried from the house and went to Nancy's car. Bess got in front with Nancy, while George seated herself in the rear. As they drove off, Bess said severely to her cousin:

"Why in the world did you talk like that to Donna Mae? Do you want to spoil everything for us? If the situation around here gets much worse, Aunt Stella and the Colonel may ask us to leave."

"I'm sorry," said George, "but Donna Mae makes me positively ill when she gets on her high horse!"

"She certainly has changed," Bess admitted.

"I'll bet Alex is putting her up to a lot of these things."

Nancy was very quiet. So many unexplained things had occurred that now she was alert for trouble at any moment.

"Cat got your tongue, Nancy?" George spoke up.

The girl detective laughed. "No," she replied, "but I have a feeling that we should be extra-cautious tonight." Then Nancy added, "I've been thinking over what you girls said about Donna Mae. She did seem very different today, especially when we were on the launch. Up to now I hadn't thought that she was interested in anything but herself. Actually, she's a very intelligent girl."

At that moment the girls reached the long, tree-lined driveway of Oleander Manor, the Bartolome estate.

Nancy began to breathe more easily. She relaxed and leaned back in her seat.

"Isn't this an attractive—?"

She never finished the sentence. From among the low branches of the tree she was just passing a stone hurtled toward her!

CHAPTER XIV

Ghost on Board

FLYING through the open car window, the large stone grazed the side of Nancy's head. It continued to the back seat, narrowly missing George, who ducked just in time to avoid injury. The rock landed with a thud against the rear cushion.

"Oh!" Bess screamed.

Nancy quickly braked the car to a stop. As the girls looked back, they saw a man running away from the tree and down the driveway.

"We must catch him!" George urged, as Nancy began to back up.

The lean stranger, realizing that he was being pursued, dashed across the lawn to some bushes and disappeared.

As Nancy opened the door to step out, Bess held her back. "Don't you dare go after him! He'll probably throw another stone."

The young detective paused, then closed the

door. Bess went on, "What a dreadful thing for him to do! Why, Nancy, you or George might have been killed, if that stone had hit you!"

"I'm afraid you're right," Nancy agreed. "Well, we'd better report it to the police right away."

As she started the car again, the girls saw Charles hurrying down the driveway toward them. He reached the car, opened the door, and jumped in beside Bess.

"Hello, everybody!" he said. "I heard you coming. How is everything?"

"Terrible," said George flatly, and told him what had happened.

The young man was aghast. "You girls sure you're all right?" he asked solicitously.

After they assured him they were, he went on, "You know, since I've been working on the showboat, I've had a couple of narrow escapes of my own. Once when I was in my car somebody shot at a tire. And—well, maybe I shouldn't tell you what happened today, or you may not want to go tonight."

"Oh, please do," Nancy begged.

Charles said that a sniper had shot at him this morning when he was on his way to the *River Princess*. "His bullet just missed me!"

"How wicked!" Bess burst out. "Oh, I hope he won't be around tonight!"

Secretly she was hoping that Nancy might can-

cel the trip, but the young detective seemed
more determined than ever to go to the *River
Princess* and solve the mystery.

"My mother mustn't know about any of these
attacks," Charles warned the girls. "So please
don't say anything."

Nancy nodded and decided not to call the
police about the stone thrower.

"You girls will be glad to know that I've provided some extra protection for you tonight.
Two friends of mine, Frank Morse and Jack
Memory, are coming to dinner and will go on the
trip with us."

"Good!" Bess said quickly. "There's safety in
numbers, especially when they're men! I feel a
lot better now!" The others laughed as they
proceeded to the house.

Mrs. Bartolome, a very attractive and charming
woman of fifty, greeted them cordially. She and
Charles took the visitors for a short stroll in their
beautiful garden, edged with boxwood. In the
bright moonlight they could see roses, delphinium
and lilies, surrounded by azalea and oleander
bushes, blooming in profusion.

"If I lived here," said Bess, breathing in deeply,
"I'd never want to leave the place. It's a divine
garden."

Mrs. Bartolome smiled, pleased by the girl's
enthusiasm. "We do love it," she said.

A few minutes later two personable young men

arrived and were introduced to the visitors: Frank Morse, slim and well-built, had blond curly hair; Jack Memory was tall and dark, with flashing mischievous brown eyes.

The dinner party proved to be a gala one. The food, which included stuffed pheasant, was delicious and the conversation humorous and sparkling.

At the end of the meal Charles announced the plan for going on the trip into the bayou.

"In order to keep our trip secret," he said, "I suggest that we stroll into the garden in pairs, then join at the rear of the garden. There's a little-used road in back of the largest rose garden and the car is hidden there."

When Nancy told Mrs. Bartolome that the girls would like to change from their dinner frocks and shoes to sports attire, their hostess led them upstairs. After showing them to a guest room, Mrs. Bartolome smiled and said, "I wish you luck in your sleuthing tonight. For Charles's sake, I'd like to see the mystery solved."

"I hope to learn a lot tonight," Nancy replied.

Quickly the girls slipped into the shirts and jeans they had brought, then joined the boys in the living room. There was a marked change in the young men's attire also. They, too, were dressed for the trip into the bayou!

As the six friends went outdoors, one of the boys commented on the brilliant full moon.

"This is fortunate," Nancy thought. "It will make traveling through that swamp easier than in total darkness." She also recalled that voodoo worshipers often held meetings when the moon was full.

Following Charles's plan, the couples separated, Nancy and Charles walking together, Bess with Frank, and George with Jack. Five minutes later they all met back of the rose garden, jumped into the car, and started off.

"So far, so good," Charles remarked, looking in his rear-view mirror. "There's no sign of anyone following us."

Two miles from the house they came to the bayou and he parked. Three canoes were hidden among the trees and bushes that overhung the water. The couples stepped in.

Bess remarked to Frank, "It's a good thing there's moonlight or you couldn't see your hand in front of your face."

"S-sh!" Nancy called across from her canoe. "We'd better keep very quiet."

The rest of the trip was made in silence. As they neared the area where the showboat was, the young people became aware of the steady beat of a tom-tom. Bess shivered a little, but Nancy, her heart pounding with excitement, sat up straighter.

A few minutes later they could distinctly hear music coming from the calliope! To herself

Nancy said, "But Charles told me the old organ could not possibly be played!"

Soon the three canoes reached the pond where the *River Princess* lay. In the moonlight, with shadows playing on her, the old craft looked unreal and spooky indeed. The music stopped at the end of a dismal tune.

Then, as if the organist had left his bench, a ghostly figure suddenly walked from the interior of the boat onto the deck. It was sheathed from head to toe in white and glided up and down as though it were floating rather than walking.

Bess clutched the sides of the canoe in which she was riding. A terrified gasp escaped her lips. As if annoyed by the sound the ghost flitted inside the old showboat.

"Shall we follow it?" Charles whispered to Nancy.

Before she could decide, a new kind of sound came from the *River Princess*—hymn chanting!

"A voodoo meeting must be going on!" Charles said in a low voice.

There was not a light on the boat and no other signs of activity. Did the strange rites take place in complete darkness with the audience sitting motionless?

Nancy leaned forward and said to her companion, "I'd like to go aboard."

Charles whispered that he thought it would be best not to go across the pond in the canoe.

A ghostly figure suddenly emerged from

"There is a stretch of moss sod on our left leading up to the boat. Suppose we find it and walk to the *River Princess*."

The three canoes came together and the directions were given to the others. Then they

the interior of the boat onto the deck

silently paddled through the shadows to the mossy walk and the girls stepped out. As their feet touched the sod, the chanting on the showboat suddenly ceased.

In the lee of a giant cypress, the girls hesi-

tated.   There was complete silence for fully ten
seconds, then they became aware of the splash of
oars.

"Someone's leaving the showboat," George remarked.

"Listen!" Nancy commanded.   A few moments later she said, "No one's leaving by canoe.
Someone is coming!"

The young people waited tensely.   From another entrance into the pond glided a rowboat.
Two figures were in it.

To the young people's complete astonishment
the couple were dressed in Colonial attire.   The
man at the oars was elderly.   The woman, about
the same age, wore a dark-colored velvet dress
and a bonnet.

The watchers were too astounded to comment.
The "Colonial gentleman" pulled up to the
River Princess.   Then he stood up and helped
the woman ascend the ladder to the deck!

CHAPTER XV

A Weird Scene

COMPLETELY mystified, Nancy and her companions watched the scene at the old showboat in awe. Why were the elderly woman and the man with her in Colonial costumes? Was she perhaps coming for some secret herbs sold at the voodoo meeting on board? And, for some reason, was the eighteenth-century attire required?

The three girls huddled together. Bess whispered that chills were going up and down her spine. "Maybe Uncle Rufus is here and is going to give the woman a treatment," she murmured.

"I wish I knew," Nancy replied. "Let's see what she does next."

The woman reached the top of the ladder and nimbly stepped over the rail. At once she walked to the entrance where theater patrons would enter if coming to see a show.

Taking a position near the doorway, the costumed, elderly woman stopped and turned toward the spot where a gangplank had once been placed. She smiled gaily, then began nodding and shaking hands as if with imaginary passengers.

"Poor thing," said Bess. "She must have lost her mind."

"It looks that way," Nancy agreed.

For nearly ten minutes the little pantomime continued. Then the woman's companion called up from the rowboat:

"Everyone's aboard, Louvina dear. The show will start soon. You've seen it so many times, honey. Suppose you come for a boat ride with me while it's going on."

The woman hesitated a few seconds and peered into the dark interior of the showboat theater.

"But there might be something new tonight," she protested.

"Oh, I think not. You'd better come now, dear. I want to show you how lovely the wild orchids near here are in the moonlight."

Finally Louvina, though obviously reluctant, came to the ladder. The elderly man assisted her in climbing down and getting into the boat.

As he started to row away, George whispered to Nancy, "Let's go ask him what's going on! He can probably solve the whole mystery in one minute."

"Wait!" Nancy said in a low voice. "I think the woman is in a trance. It might be disastrous to awaken her. I'd rather follow the two of them and find out what I can from the man later when he's alone."

"I guess you're right," George agreed.

Despite his age, the elderly man was a swift rower and the boat was soon out of sight.

The girls stepped back into their canoes and in whispered tones talked the matter over with their escorts.

"Somebody should stay here and watch the *River Princess*," Nancy declared. "Are any of you willing to go aboard?"

Frank and Jack were eager to, but insisted that Bess and George remain outside in the canoes.

"No point in you girls taking any unnecessary chances," Frank said, and Bess gave him a grateful look.

In the end it was decided that only Nancy and Charles would follow the mysterious couple.

Charles paddled swiftly in pursuit. Soon only about a hundred yards separated the two crafts.

"Do you want me to overtake them?" Charles asked Nancy in a low voice.

"No," she replied quietly. "Just keep them in sight. I'd like to find out where they're going. It may have something to do with the mystery."

The stream was so overgrown with weeds that it was difficult to find a clear passageway. But apparently the man in Colonial costume knew his way perfectly. Nancy concluded that he must be a native of the area.

"I wonder who he and Louvina are," Nancy asked herself. "The woman may have been an actress and—oh, ouch!"

The tangled growth pulled at Nancy's hair and whipped her face as Charles wound his way in and out among the lush vegetation. Once they lost the elderly couple completely. But finally the canoe emerged from the tangled mass into an open stream.

"Do you see the couple?" Nancy asked, turning around to look at him.

"No—yes, I do. They're over on the right and way ahead."

Fortunately, the moon went under a cloud at this moment. Nancy said she wished they might slip up unobserved and perhaps hear the couple's plans.

"I'll try to get closer," Charles said. In the dim light he almost overtook the strange pair and after that followed more cautiously.

A few minutes later it became apparent that the oarsman was heading for a dock concealed in a small cove. Nancy and Charles came very close, so they would not lose their quarry when the man and woman debarked.

Some distance from the dock, at the end of a small flower garden, stood a modest house. A few lights gleamed in the windows and a small lamp at the door was turned on.

As the rowboat reached the dock, Louvina stood up. Taking a step forward, she bent down to kiss her companion. Then, as he helped her, she stepped to the dock.

In a sweet, musical voice she said, "Thank you so very much, Henry. The show was delightful, wasn't it? Have a good night's sleep, dear. And do come over soon. I'll be expecting you."

"Yes, honey, I will."

Without another word the woman tripped girlishly up the walk through the garden and entered the house.

" 'Henry' doesn't live here after all," Nancy told herself.

The elderly gentleman sat staring after Louvina. When she turned off the door light, he stepped from the rowboat and tied the painter to a post. Then he, too, started up the walk.

"Oh, please wait a minute!" Nancy called to him. "I'd like to talk with you."

Charles pulled up to the dock and she stepped out of the canoe. The elderly man, startled, turned around. A look of fright gave way to one of amazement upon seeing a smiling girl standing there.

"I'm sorry if I frightened you," Nancy said. "Please forgive me. I just wanted to ask you—"

Henry did not seem to be paying attention.

He was staring at his costume. Embarrassed, he interrupted her to say, "Please pardon my attire. There's a special reason why I'm wearing it!"

By this time Charles was also standing on the dock. He apologized for his and Nancy's intrusion, then said, "It's very important that we talk to you. This is Nancy Drew from River Heights. I'm Charles Bartolome. I live not very far from here. Perhaps you know my family."

"Yes, I do. Now what do you wish to ask me?" the elderly man inquired.

Nancy began to talk. First she told him about having seen him and his companion at the *River Princess*. Henry looked startled.

"The *River Princess* is on Colonel Haver's property, as you may know," she said. "He has asked me to try to solve the mystery of it. Can you tell me why people think the showboat is haunted?"

Henry looked searchingly at the girl's face. Then he smiled. "I'll tell you the whole story."

CHAPTER XVI

Lost in the Bayou

"MY NAME," said the elderly man in the Colonial costume, "is Henry de la Verne. Louvina is my twin. Her married name is Mrs. Claibourne Farwell. She is a widow now."

As he paused, Nancy suggested kindly, "Shall we sit down?"

"Perhaps that would be best," said Mr. de la Verne. He led Nancy and Charles to a quaint little summerhouse in the garden.

After they were seated on a bench across from his, the man went on:

"This will no doubt surprise you, but our grandfather owned the *River Princess*. As children, Louvina and I spent a great deal of time on her." Again Mr. de la Verne paused and smiled reflectively, as if this brought back happy memories.

Charles remarked, "It must have been a great deal of fun, sir, for you and your sister."

"Indeed it was," Henry agreed. "Louvina loved to play actress and try on the various costumes. She always planned to act on the *River Princess* when she was older, but never had a chance. There was a great storm and flood which drove the showboat to her present location and she was abandoned. Our grandfather died of shock and injuries he received during the storm."

"How tragic!" Nancy murmured, deeply touched.

"Yes, it was, and the whole thing made a tremendous impression on my sister. She was very upset about the fate of our beloved grandfather and showboat, but as Louvina grew older, the family thought she had forgotten the episode. She married happily and lived a very normal life.

"But after Mr. Farwell's sudden death several years ago," Mr. de la Verne went on, "Louvina's mind began to play tricks on her. She started living more and more with her memories. Finally, I came to stay with my sister after I retired, and help her with her business affairs." He smiled. "I'm a bachelor."

After another pause, he said, "I humor Louvina all I can. We were very close as children, playing together almost constantly."

Mr. de la Verne looked up at the sky. The clouds had been blown past and the moon was shining brightly again.

"On nights when there's a full moon my sister's mind always reverts to her childhood. It's then she insists that the two of us put on costumes which our grandparents used to wear, and go to the *River Princess*."

Nancy and Charles smiled understandingly and Nancy murmured, "You are very wonderful, Mr. de la Verne, to be so patient and thoughtful."

The man suddenly chuckled. "It is a good thing that Louvina picks moonlight nights for our trips. Otherwise I could never find my way to the showboat." After a few seconds he added, "Well, that is my story. Does it clear up the mystery of the supposedly haunted showboat for you?"

"Partly," Nancy replied, "and thank you very much for confiding in us, Mr. de la Verne. "I'd like to ask you a few questions if I may. I'm dreadfully sorry to hear of your sister's trouble, but I'm sure she is not unhappy."

"Oh, no," Henry answered quickly. "As a matter of fact, she is happier when she is playing a part than when her memory serves her normally. Then she starts worrying about me."

"Mr. de la Verne," Nancy said, "yesterday I found an antique ornamental hairpin on the deck of the *River Princess*." She described it, and added, "Does it, by any chance, belong to your sister?"

"Why, yes, it does," Henry answered. "She

insisted upon wearing it to the showboat on one of her trips. It must have dropped out of her hair."

"I'll return it soon," Nancy offered, then said, "Tonight we heard a tom-tom being beaten and calliope music playing on the *River Princess*. And we actually saw a ghostly figure parading up and down the deck just before you and your sister arrived!"

"What!" Henry cried out.

"It's true," Charles spoke up. "The figure disappeared inside the showboat when you drew near."

The elderly man was visibly disturbed. He said quickly that Louvina must not know about this—it would certainly upset her. And hereafter, when he took her there, he would make certain no one was around.

"I thought, of course, we were alone," he said worriedly.

"Then you have no idea who might be visiting the showboat?" Nancy asked.

"None whatever. I have heard a tom-tom being beaten in the bayou," the man confessed. "But I thought the drummer was some Negro who had inherited the instrument from an African ancestor. As to the calliope, I cannot understand it. The old organ is in no condition to be played."

Nancy asked Mr. de la Verne if he thought

secret voodoo meetings were being held on the *River Princess.*

"It's possible. Such a thing never occurred to me."

"Do you know Uncle Rufus?" Nancy asked. When the elderly man nodded, she asked, "Do you think he could be leading the meetings?"

Mr. de la Verne vetoed this possibility. "Uncle Rufus is a fine, highly respected man in this neighborhood. He does a great deal of good; he certainly would not conduct any such secret meetings. By the way, why are you interested in solving the mystery of the haunted showboat?"

Nancy told him about the plans for moving it and the forthcoming ball the Havers were giving.

"Move it?" Mr. de la Verne cried out. "Oh, if that is done, it will kill my sister!"

"But if there *should* be any danger on the *River Princess,* you would not wish Mrs. Farwell to go aboard it," Nancy pointed out.

"Yes, that is true," the man admitted. "Perhaps if we are careful, there will be no trouble."

"I wonder," said Nancy. "Mr. de la Verne, do you know of any reason why persons other than voodoo worshipers might want to make the showboat appear to be haunted? Or to sabotage it?"

Before replying the elderly man stood up. For several seconds he looked off into space, then said:

"Yes, there might be. But that is a family matter. I cannot tell you about it. But one thing I'm sure of. It would be very foolish for Colonel Haver to try moving the *River Princess!*"

Bowing, Henry de la Verne abruptly said good night and hurried up the garden walk to the house.

"Good night," the young people called.

As Nancy looked after the man, she mulled over his sentence. What *was* the rest of the story he was not willing to tell? And was he trying to send a message to Colonel Haver, by way of Nancy, that it would be dangerous for the owner of Sunnymead to continue his efforts to have the old boat moved?

As she and Charles stepped into their canoe, Nancy mentioned these thoughts to her companion. He smiled. "The old gentleman certainly makes it sound ominous. Maybe we'll find a skeleton hidden away some place on the showboat!"

Nancy laughed. "Perhaps a family skeleton!"

Charles paddled quickly and soon reached the tangled mass of bayou growth through which they must pass to reach the *River Princess*. Once more the moon went under a cloud. It was pitch black in the swamp, but Charles continued to paddle, with Nancy ducking when leaves and stems brushed her head.

"I've got to give you credit for following a good hunch, Nancy," Charles said admiringly. "I like a girl with initiative. If it hadn't been for Donna Mae's—" He broke off abruptly.

Nancy thought, "I have *another* hunch! Charles is still in love with Donna Mae, even if she has hurt his pride." But she felt it best, under the circumstances, not to make any comment.

There was a long silence, broken only by the ripple of water from the canoe paddles. Then Nancy laughed softly. "Charles, you're absolutely amazing the way you can see in the dark!"

"Don't praise me too soon," he replied. "1 have a feeling I'm off course completely."

Five minutes later he confessed that he was lost. "From the length of time that I've been paddling, we should be at the showboat."

Charles offered to try yelling to their friends to see if they could get directions. But Nancy felt that this might be a dangerous move. If any of their enemies were around, it would pinpoint the canoe's location.

"Why don't we go back to the open water near Mr. de la Verne's house and then start over again," she suggested.

"It won't hurt to try," Charles replied.

But the longer he paddled the more hopelessly lost he became in the moss-draped swamp. Finally Charles said, "We'll have to give it up and wait for daylight."

Back at the showboat, Bess, George, and the two boys were becoming frantic over the long absence of their friends. Three hours had gone by and still Nancy and Charles had not returned.

"Oh, I just know something terrible has happened to them!" Bess wailed.

"Don't say such things!" George chided her cousin. "You know Nancy when she's sleuthing. She just won't give up."

"Let's continue our search of the showboat," Frank suggested to distract the girls from worrying.

The young people had already discovered several places in the walls and floors which had been hacked since the day before. But there had been no further sign of the ghostly figure, nor any more voodoo sounds or calliope music since Nancy and Charles had departed.

Now they gathered near the stairway that led to the hold of the old river vessel. George gazed down into it, then turned around.

"Maybe something valuable is hidden on this boat!" she said.

As she said this, George stepped back. Without warning the top step of the stairway, evidently rotted, gave way. She plunged into the inky blackness below!

CHAPTER XVII

The Towboat Captain

"OH, GEORGE!" Bess screamed, looking down into the hold for some sign of her cousin.

Bess carried a flashlight and now tried to focus it into the black depths. Her hand shook and she could not hold the light steady. There was no answer to her cry. The young people were fearful that George had been badly injured.

"I'll go down and see what happened," Frank offered. Picking his way carefully down the steps, he found the girl lying in a huddled heap some feet from the base of the stairway.

"George! George!" he called, sloshing through muddy water to reach her.

He leaned down and gently lifted her up. She seemed dazed, but was able to stand. "Wh— what happened?" George asked shakily.

"You took a header," Frank replied. "I'll help you up the stairs."

Bess, almost tearful with relief, and Jack

reached down to assist the couple. The four young people walked out on the deck and Frank offered to take George home at once.

"Oh, I'll be all right," she said gamely. "Nothing hurts but my leg and I can stand that." She would not hear of leaving the showboat until Nancy and Charles returned.

The group sat down on the deck and discussed the mystery. As dawn broke, they began to worry anew about the missing couple.

"We *must* do something to find Nancy and Charles," Bess insisted.

Frank and Jack offered to take a canoe and try to locate them. "I guess you girls will be all right here alone in the daylight," Jack remarked.

Just as they were about to leave, another canoe suddenly appeared.

"Nancy! Charles!" the others shouted in relief.

"I guess you all thought we were lost," Charles called. "Well, we were!"

Stories were quickly exchanged. The four who had stayed on the showboat were amazed to learn about Henry and Louvina. After telling them that Mr. de la Verne had hinted at some family secret in connection with the haunted showboat, Charles repeated his guess that there might be a skeleton aboard.

Jack laughed. "And it's his ghost we saw walking around? Let's look for old Bonesy."

But Bess insisted that the group leave at once.

"We can come back another time. I'm worried about what the Havers will say."

Charles smiled. "Don't worry. Mother will take care of that."

"I'm sure she will," said Nancy. "And, George, if you feel all right. I'd like to stay here a little while and look around the boat myself. Let's see if we can find out what the De la Vernes' secret is."

The young people spent another hour in an intensive search. Nancy even went down into the hold and flashed her light around. There were a few inches of water on the low side where the boat had listed. In the dry section they found no clue to anything hidden there. Nancy said she was ready to leave, so she and Charles joined the others.

"I inspected that old calliope very thoroughly," Frank spoke up. "Couldn't get a sound out of it. How do you all explain its being played?"

Nancy thought for a few moments, then replied, "I believe someone comes aboard with a record player and plays calliope music and hymns."

"And the tom-tom, too?" George asked. "He's got quite a record collection!"

The others laughed, then Jack asked Nancy if she thought the person who did these things had been hired by someone or was actually the saboteur.

"I don't know," the young detective replied. "But I've been wondering if there is some mechanism a distance from the showboat that triggers an alarm. That would account for all the sounds on the *River Princess* stopping just before the De la Vernes showed up."

Charles suggested that the boys make a search in the waterways leading to the showboat. The girls waited on deck while they took the three canoes and scouted around. Twenty minutes later they returned and reported that nothing had been found.

"Then the men probably use the birdcalls or some other bayou sound as signals," Nancy decided.

Jack looked at the girl intently. "If so, this means that there may be spies around all the time."

"Probably it does," Nancy agreed. "And it may also mean that there's not much point in our being so secretive."

Frank laughed. "Well, then, all we have to do is find the spies and the mystery will be solved!"

Nancy chuckled. "Right!" To herself she added, "And I'm going to enlist Uncle Rufus's aid to do this."

When the three couples reached Charles's home, Mrs. Bartolome was greatly relieved to see them.

"I was mighty worried about you all," she said. "But I didn't want to upset Mrs. Haver, so I phoned and told her you girls were staying all night."

Nancy and Charles related the entire story. Mrs. Bartolome was particularly interested in learning about Mrs. Farwell and her brother.

"I knew them fairly well years ago," she said. "I thought that after Mr. Farwell died, his widow had moved away. I'm dreadfully sorry to learn that her mind is no longer completely sound."

"Have you any idea what the family secret in connection with the showboat may be?" Nancy asked Charles's mother.

Mrs. Bartolome shook her head. "Surely it can't be anything disgraceful. The De la Vernes were very fine people. Henry is a graduate of Oxford in England."

Charles's mother went on to say that Henry had always been intensely interested in the university and its activities, although he had graduated many, many years ago.

Changing the subject, she said, "You all must be starving. We'll have breakfast at once."

Because of the early hour the servants were still asleep, so the group gathered in the kitchen and prepared orange juice, bacon and eggs, toast and cocoa themselves.

Mrs. Bartolome caught Bess stifling a yawn. "Wouldn't you girls like to sleep for a while before you return to the Havers?" she asked solicitously.

They all confessed that they would. After Frank and Jack had said good-by, the three girls went to the guest rooms and slept soundly for four hours. Then they put on their dinner frocks and left for Sunnymead.

As Nancy parked her car there, Donna Mae rushed out to meet them. "My goodness!" she exclaimed. "You really made a visit! Tell me about everything!"

"To begin with," Nancy said, "we had a perfectly delicious dinner and breakfast."

"The Bartolomes' gardens are absolutely heavenly," Bess added. "I thoroughly enjoyed my walk in them."

George grinned impishly. "Oh, don't be so stingy with your information, girls. Donna Mae, two charming boys came to join us. Maybe you know them—Frank Morris and Jack Memory."

"Oh, yes, I know them," Donna Mae replied. "Did you spend the whole evening with them?"

"The whole evening," Nancy replied.

"Well, for goodness sake, tell me about it!" Donna Mae begged. As they walked toward the house, Donna Mae suddenly noticed that George was limping. "Oh, dear! What happened to you?"

"Oh, just a little spill," George answered noncommittally.

"Where?" Donna Mae asked pointedly.

"On a stairway," George replied. "Clumsy of me, wasn't it?"

Donna Mae was silent for a few seconds. She asked no more questions. Apparently she had decided that her friends were not going to tell any more about their evening at the Bartolomes'.

Suddenly Donna Mae smiled and said, "I have some great news for you girls. You won't have to date Charles and his friends. I've phoned Ned Nickerson. He's coming to the Mardi Gras and bringing Burt and Dave with him."

"Hypers!" George exclaimed. "They're really coming?"

"They sure are," Donna Mae answered. "I told you they would," she added smugly.

She insisted that the girls change their clothes at once, so that the whole group could go downtown to pick out costumes for Ned and his friends to wear to the ball.

"Everything must be perfect." she said. "I don't know your friends' sizes. So you girls will have to pick out the costumes."

Nancy was disappointed that she could not get in touch with Uncle Rufus immediately. "But," she consoled herself, "on second thought, perhaps I can do a little detective work in New Orleans instead."

Inside the house the girls found Alex starting to dismantle the living room. Pappy Cole was carrying out furniture and Mammy Matilda was taking down draperies.

Mrs. Haver seemed to be flustered and upset about the whole thing. Sighing, she said, "Oh dear, I *do* wish the showboat could be moved here and this room not disturbed."

Nancy agreed. Suddenly an idea came to her. She saw Colonel Haver in the garden and went out to speak to him. She inquired whether every towboat captain in the area had been approached and asked if he could move the *River Princess*.

"Well, I suppose so," the Colonel replied. "Alex attended to that and I'm sure he would have exhausted every means."

Nancy began to wonder whether Alex Upgrove *had* "exhausted every means." She decided to make a few inquiries of her own while in the city. There would still be time for the *River Princess* to be moved before the Havers' ball!

George begged off from the trip because her leg was sore and bruised.

Nancy and Bess changed into smart cotton knit suits. A short time later the girls drove off with Donna Mae in Nancy's car. Within an hour they had selected three different clown suits for the boys from Emerson College.

"Before we start home," Nancy said to Donna Mae, as they were leaving the costumer's, "I'd like to drive down to the waterfront."

Donna Mae agreed, so Nancy headed for the docks. As she drove past the many wharves, the young sleuth looked intently for any towboats that might be moored there. Presently she came to one and stopped.

"I want to run in here a minute," she said. "Be right back. Wait in the car, will you?"

Fortunately, the towboat owner, a Captain Runcie, was on board. Nancy inquired if he had ever been asked to move the stranded *River Princess*. When he said no, she told him about the ball and the Havers' plans.

"Captain Runcie, would you consider trying to tow the showboat out of the bayou?" Nancy asked.

"I'll be glad to look her over and let you know."

"Then could you come to the Haver home and talk to the Colonel?"

"I'll be there early tomorrow morning," Captain Runcie promised.

"Thank you very much," said Nancy. "We'll be looking for you."

When she returned to the car, Nancy said nothing about her errand because she felt Donna Mae might be upset to learn that Alex had not explored every possibility in having the old boat moved. At once the girl complained about Nancy's secrecy.

The young dectective merely laughed and said, "I'm full of secrets, all right. But I'll let you in on one. My next stop will be the police station."

"Oh!" Donna Mae cried out. "Why?"

"I still hope to track down my stolen car," Nancy replied.

When they reached police headquarters, she went inside alone and introduced herself to the captain in charge. "Is there any news about my missing car or the man who stole it?" she asked.

"No, there isn't, Miss Drew," the captain replied. "But we do have a little news that may be a clue. My men made a thorough search of the room that fellow rented. In it they found a suitcase full of women's clothes."

"A suitcase?" Nancy exclaimed. "Maybe it's my stolen bag!"

CHAPTER XVIII

The Simmering Caldron

THE POLICE captain looked at Nancy in surprise. "Your suitcase?"

Nancy explained that a suitcase of hers had been in the luggage compartment of her stolen car. "Were there any initials on the bag you found?" she asked.

"There had been," the officer replied. "They'd been scratched off."

Nancy asked to see the bag. Using his desk phone, the captain requested a sergeant to bring the suitcase to his office.

Upon seeing it, Nancy cried out, "It is mine! Oh, I hope my mother's fan and shawl are still inside!"

Quickly she lifted the lid. Her clothes were intact. Rummaging among them she found that the heirlooms were there.

"Oh, I'm so relieved!" she said happily. "I'd rather lose my car than this shawl and fan!"

The captain smiled understandingly. "I'm glad that we could recover them for you," he said. "But actually it was you, Miss Drew, who discovered the house where the suitcase was hidden."

At that moment the officer's phone rang and he picked up the receiver. After listening a few moments, he put down the instrument and turned to Nancy.

"Well, this seems to be your day for recovering things. Your stolen car has been found in an out-of-town secondhand lot."

"Oh, how wonderful!" Nancy exclaimed.

The captain went on to say that the man who had brought the car in had given the name Ralph Winter and said he came from New York City. "He had a bill of sale, so naturally the lot man did not suspect the car had been stolen."

"If it *is* my car," said Nancy, "then the bill of sale must have been forged."

"You're quite right," the captain agreed. "The car is yours, all right. My man checked the serial numbers."

"Was the thief caught?" Nancy asked.

"Not yet," the officer answered. "But we'll send out an alarm. The man bought a gray sedan."

"Did my description of the car thief fit this man?" Nancy inquired.

"Yes, it did—dark, slender, forty years old.

Small, piercing black eyes. Low forehead, hair rather coarse and stiff."

Nancy smiled. "He's the one, all right." She thanked the captain for all his help and left headquarters.

When Nancy appeared at the car carrying her suitcase, Bess's eyes grew large. "Your stolen bag!" she said unbelievingly. "Is everything in it?"

"Everything," Nancy answered. Turning to Donna Mae, she said, "Even my mother's shawl and fan, which I can now use at the ball."

"I know you will look simply adorable!" Donna Mae cried out ecstatically.

On the way home Nancy announced that she would like to stop at Uncle Rufus's cabin. Donna Mae became a little impatient. She wanted to hurry home and talk with Alex.

"Oh, I shan't be long," Nancy promised her.

When they reached the tiny cabin in the bayou, no one was around. Nancy suggested that the other girls wait in the car while she looked to see if the old man was in the rear of his property. She had detected the smell of smoke and thought that Uncle Rufus might be burning brush.

As the young sleuth rounded the corner of the house, she stood still in amazement. In the center of the yard a large tripod had been erected over a log fire. Swinging from the tripod was a huge iron caldron. Back of it stood Uncle Rufus, waving his arms back and forth slowly and muttering to himself.

Nancy hesitated about interrupting the voodoo preacher-doctor. He probably was brewing a potion from herbs and uttering prayers for its success and efficacy whenever it might be used by his patients.

It was fully two minutes before Uncle Rufus looked up. Seeing Nancy, he left his work and walked toward her. "Good day," he said affably. "I 'spects you wonder what's in this here herb pot." The elderly man chuckled. "It's a secret, but effen you need a tonic, it'll fix you up right quick."

Nancy smiled. "I'll let you know if I need one."

She told Uncle Rufus she had stopped to ask him if he would do some detective work for her.

He grinned. "If you *con*-fine it to the bayou, I will," he said.

"Oh, I will," Nancy promised.

She went on to tell him about the weird scenes and sounds on the *River Princess* but did not mention the part that the De la Vernes had played. She watched the old man's face intently to see if he showed any signs of guilt. He definitely did not. Instead, he scratched his head and looked perplexed.

"This here is a big puzzlement to me," he said. "Once in a while I hear a tom-tom, but

Uncle Rufus was waving his arms and muttering

lots of our folks got *them*. I'se sure none of those people goes near that ole showboat."

Nancy mentioned the fact that perhaps some people were using a record player there.

"Maybe so." Uncle Rufus nodded. "But none of my people," he denied stoutly. "Maybe I do know somethin', though, that might help you. Last night when I was out paddlin' I stopped to listen to an ole owl. He's wisdom, you know, an' I thought I might learn somethin' from him."

Uncle Rufus went on to say that a short distance from him he had heard two men speaking. He was sure from their accents that they were white men from the North.

"What they said was kind o' queerlike. One said, 'I guess the old gal hasn't any pirate gold after all.' The other man said, 'I'm goin' to keep at her till I find out!'"

Uncle Rufus asked Nancy if she could figure out what they meant, but the young detective shook her head. "That's a hard one," she said. Then she asked, "Uncle Rufus, would it be possible for you to watch the showboat for a few nights? If you learn anything, come to the Havers' home and tell me."

The voodoo doctor smiled. "That will be easy detective work," he said, chuckling. "Is that all you want me to do, Miss Nancy?"

"That's all for now. And thank you very much."

She hurried back to the car and told the others what the old man was doing. "He's a great character in these parts," Donna Mae said. "It's said that Uncle Rufus has brought about a good many cures."

When the girls reached Sunnymead, George was waiting for them on the patio. Donna Mae went off to find Alex, and George gestured that she would like Nancy and Bess to follow her at once to the second floor.

"I wonder what's up," Nancy thought as she mounted the staircase.

George led the way into Nancy's bedroom and closed the door. "Well, I think I've really picked up a good clue," she said.

Excitedly George went on to say that she had spent almost an hour with Alex. "I got him to talk about New York, his travels and his education. He showed me a lot of pictures."

"But what's the clue?" Bess asked impatiently.

George looked intently at the two girls as she replied, "I think Alex Upgrove is a fake!"

"What!" Nancy and Bess exclaimed.

"I mean it," George went on. "In our talk I tried to trip him and I think I succeeded. He contradicted himself several times. I'm convinced he's either posing as Alex Upgrove from New York or else his name *is* Alex Upgrove, but he's claiming a position of wealth and social standing to which he isn't entitled."

George opened a bureau drawer and brought out a picture. "Much as I hate flattery, I used some of it on Alex and got him to let me borrow this picture." She made a wry face. "I think he believes I have a crush on him."

Nancy and Bess stifled giggles, then looked at the photograph. It showed a group of students at Oxford University.

George pointed to one in the rear row. "That's Alex Upgrove," she explained. "Is he the man who's going to marry Donna Mae or did he help himself to this picture of someone who looks very much like him?"

"Well, it certainly looks like him," Bess said.

"Yes, it does," said Nancy. Then she snapped her fingers. "I have an idea. You remember Mrs. Bartolome telling us that Mr. de la Verne is an Oxford graduate and has always kept up his interest in the university?"

"Yes," said George, "but Alex would have been at Oxford long after Mr. de la Verne. How could he identify the person in this picture?"

"I know it's a long shot," said Nancy. "But Mr. de la Verne may have other pictures or records of Oxford graduates. Let's go see him, with the excuse that we're returning Mrs. Farwell's ornamental hairpin."

Nancy looked at her wrist watch. "If we hurry, girls, we can just make the trip before dinner. Come on!"

CHAPTER XIX

A Missing Suspect

To AVOID meeting Alex or any of the Haver family, Nancy, Bess, and George slipped quietly down the back stairs and left the mansion. They hurried to their car and drove to Mrs. Farwell's home.

Nancy rang the bell and Mr. de la Verne opened the door. He bowed, then said:

"This is an unexpected pleasure. Please come in."

The girls stepped inside and Nancy introduced the elderly man to her friends. After greeting them, he indicated a small living room filled with beautiful antique mahogany furniture. When they were seated, Nancy drew the jeweled hairpin from her purse.

"I came to return this," she said.

Henry de la Verne hesitated a moment, then

arose. "My sister is not too well today, but I will see if she is able to join us."

He was gone fully five minutes, but at last returned with Mrs. Farwell. Though her face was lined and her eyes slightly dulled because of her failing health, she was still a very pretty woman. The girls were touched by the affectionate and chivalrous manner with which her brother treated her. The callers arose and he introduced them. Mrs. Farwell nodded her head graciously as each girl was named.

"I found one of your valued possessions, Mrs. Farwell," said Nancy. "I'm so happy to be able to return it to you."

Louvina Farwell took the proffered hairpin and stared at it for several seconds. Then she stood up very straight, gave a little toss of her head, and looked directly at the girl detective. To Nancy's astonishment, the woman's eyes indicated she was perfectly rational.

"Do sit down again, my dears," urged Mrs. Farwell. After her brother had helped seat her in a chair, the woman asked, "And where did you find my missing heirloom, Nancy?"

"On the old showboat, the *River Princess*."

"How very odd!" Louvina remarked. "I feel so sorry about the *River Princess*. Henry and I had such wonderful times on it when we were children. It is too bad that storm and flood ruined it."

"Would you like to see the *River Princess* restored and moved out of the bayou?" George asked.

"Indeed I would," Mrs. Farwell replied promptly. "And I would like to see performances given on it again." She turned to her brother. "Wouldn't it be fun, Henry, to go to one of those old-time shows again?"

"Yes, it would," Henry replied. He gave Nancy a surprised glance, as if to say, "I was all wrong about the effect on my sister of the restoration of the *River Princess*."

Nancy, encouraged by the friendly trend of the conversation, asked impulsively, "Before your grandfather owned the showboat, did pirates ever pilot her?"

"Oh, no," Henry answered quickly. Then, as his sister started to speak, he tried to switch to another topic of discussion.

But Louvina would not be diverted from the pirate story. She laughed as if in recollection and her eyes lost some of their dimness. She said, "Nancy, my dear, no pirate ever owned the *River Princess*. But there was a story that several of them hid a chest of gold coins under a bulkhead of the showboat during the time my grandfather owned it. This happened when no one was aboard."

"Oh, how exciting!" Bess burst out. "Did they return to get them?"

"Not that anyone ever knew," Mrs. Farwell replied. "As a matter of fact, some very disparaging remarks were made about my wonderful grandfather—people said that he was in league with the pirates."

"Why, how dreadful!" said Bess.

"It certainly was," Mr. de la Verne agreed. "Well, now that my sister has told you of our family skeleton, I'll finish the story. I myself looked for that pirate gold many times before the *River Princess* was abandoned, but it never came to light."

Nancy was convinced now that at last she had discovered the reason for the showboat's being "haunted." At the present time, someone who had learned of the old story was trying to find the pirate gold—and did not intend to have anyone interfere with his endeavor!

"Just today," Nancy said aloud, "I asked Uncle Rufus to watch the *River Princess* at night and report to me anything strange he saw going on there. He overheard a remark in which I think you'll be interested."

The young detective told about the two men in the canoe and their mention of pirate gold.

"I'm sure they'll never find it," said Henry de la Verne, "because the whole story probably was made up by some showboat rivals of my grandfather's."

Louvina backed up her brother in this theory.

Then, suddenly, she said, "I am very tired. If the girls will excuse me, I think I'll go to my room and lie down."

"Oh, please do," said Nancy quickly. "But Mr. de la Verne, may we stay a little longer and talk to you? I want to ask you some questions about Oxford University."

"I shall be happy to answer them," the elderly man said with enthusiasm. "I'll be back in a few minutes." He assisted his sister from the room but returned shortly.

Briefly, Nancy told about Alex Upgrove, and that his engagement to Donna Mae Haver was to be announced at a ball the Havers were giving.

"Here is a picture of Alex taken at Oxford. I was wondering if you could find him in your directory of graduates."

The elderly man took the photograph. Then he ushered the visitors into an adjoining room which was lined with bookshelves, and pulled out several volumes. Presently he announced to the girls that an Alex Upgrove from New York City was indeed a graduate of Oxford University.

Mr. de la Verne then looked through a volume of pictures. This book was put back on the shelf, and he took down another. Presently he exclaimed:

"I've found what you're looking for!"

The girls eagerly crowded around him and looked at the group photograph. It was exactly like the one which George had borrowed from Alex Upgrove. But the face of the man who stood in the place indicated for Alex was not that of the man they knew at Sunnymead.

"George, you were right about Alex being a fake!" Bess cried out.

"This is very unfortunate," said Mr. de la Verne.

Nancy raised her head thoughtfully. As she stared out a window, she was startled by a face framed in one of the panes.

Alex Upgrove!

When the young man realized that Nancy had caught him spying, he took to his heels and sprinted out of sight. Nancy alerted the others and the three girls dashed from the house after him. A few minutes later the roar of a car some distance away told them that he had escaped.

"I'll bet he'll never show up at Sunnymead again," George predicted.

"Well, that's fine with me," Bess declared. "And I'm glad for Donna Mae's sake that he's been found out. Maybe now she'll come to her senses and be her former self!"

They returned to the house and apologized to Mr. de la Verne for their hasty exit.

"I'm sorry you didn't catch up with that pretender," he said. "I will notify the university of what has happened. While you were gone, I studied the photograph you brought, under a magnifying glass. There has been a very clever photographic substitution."

"This Alex Upgrove, if that's his name," said George, "must be after big stakes to have gone to so much trouble."

"I'll bet he's after the pirate gold," Bess ventured.

The girls thanked Mr. de la Verne for his help, then said good-by and hurried back toward Sunnymead.

"How in the world are we ever going to tell Donna Mae the truth?" Bess asked apprehensively.

"Maybe we won't have to," Nancy suggested. "She may find out about Alex herself."

When the girls drove into the parking area of the Havers' estate, they gave gasps of surprise and delight. On the patio with Donna Mae were three boys—tall, athletic, brown-eyed Ned Nickerson; blond, heavy-set Burt Eddleton, and rangy-built, green-eyed Dave Evans. The girls hurried to greet them.

"We convinced the university we ought to look over the football situation down here for next year," Ned said with a laugh after greetings were over.

"And it happened to coincide with a midyear vacation." Burt grinned.

In the conversation which followed, Nancy noticed that Donna Mae was unusually charming and gracious. She exhibited such happiness that the other girls were sure she had heard nothing adverse yet about Alex Upgrove. And how they hated to tell her!

Suddenly Donna Mae announced, "Dinner will be served soon. We won't wait for Alex. He had to go out and said he might be detained."

The girls exchanged quick glances but made no comment. Excusing themselves, they hurried upstairs to change into flowered bouffant dresses.

"For the sake of Ned, Burt, and Dave," said Nancy, as she and the others started downstairs, "I suggest that we be as gay as possible during dinner. If Alex doesn't show up later on, then we'll have to tell Donna Mae what we've learned about him."

Though at times it was difficult for the three girls to play their lighthearted parts, they succeeded very well. But later, on the terrace, Colonel and Mrs. Haver brought up the subject of Alex.

"Where did he go?" they asked their daughter.

Donna Mae said she did not know. Another hour went by. Still he did not come.

Nancy took Ned aside and whispered the news about Alex. "If you don't mind, I'd like to tell the Havers privately what I know."

Ned chuckled. "I can take a hint," he said, grinning. "I might have known you'd have a big mystery to solve. Okay, we fellows will hit the sack."

Presently he and his friends excused themselves and went upstairs. Donna Mae fidgeted, then said worriedly, "I can't understand where Alex is."

Nancy decided not to wait any longer in revealing what she had discovered. She walked over to Donna Mae and her parents. "I'm afraid that Alex is not coming back," she said gently. "Bess and George and I learned earlier this evening that he has been misrepresenting his background. He was there when we found it out and he ran away."

"What do you mean?" Donna Mae asked quickly.

Nancy told about the substitution in the photograph. Colonel Haver's jaw set firmly. Donna Mae went white and the others thought she was going to faint. But suddenly she began to cry.

"That d-dreadful, that deceiving, that horrid man!" she burst out.

Mrs. Haver, who was seated beside Donna Mae, put an arm around her daughter. "This is hard, I know, dear, but think of the disgrace and unhappiness for you if you had married a person like that. We all have probably been spared a great deal of embarrassment, too."

Her mother's words made little impression

on Donna Mae. She could think of nothing but the overwhelming chagrin of the moment. As she alternately wept and laughed hysterically, her father asked Nancy if she thought Alex was in any way connected with the mystery of the showboat.

"I'm afraid that he is," the young detective replied. "In fact, I am convinced Alex is in league with the man who stole my car. And that many other strange things which happened were meant to keep me from coming here to solve the mystery."

"But what *is* the mystery?" Colonel Haver asked.

Nancy told him of the rumor about pirate gold being hidden on the *River Princess*. The Havers were amazed to hear this. They eagerly discussed the possibility of the ancient coins being on the showboat. Donna Mae momentarily forgot her troubles and even joined in the conversation.

But as the group started for bed, she again broke into another fit of hysteria. Nancy went to Donna Mae's room with her and tried to soothe the agitated girl.

To the young detective's wonder, Donna Mae revealed a new worry. "Nancy, I've just realized what a dreadful thing I've done to Charles, and he didn't deserve it."

Although Nancy felt sorry for the girl, and was

sure Donna Mae still loved Charles, she was a little irked at her fickleness. Nevertheless, she endeavored to comfort Donna Mae, who finally fell asleep.

The next morning Donna Mae appeared quite composed. She talked very little during breakfast, but later asked the three girls to come to her room. To their surprise and relief, Donna Mae seemed to have a more mature attitude.

"I've been very stupid," she said. "All this has taught me a good lesson. I know now that I still love Charles—and have all the time. I shan't go running after him. But if he'll take me back, I'll be very happy."

The girls had no chance to comment, for just then Mammy Matilda knocked on the door to say that Captain Runcie, the towboat owner, was downstairs. "Colonel Haver would like you all to come and talk with him."

When they reached the first floor, Colonel Haver said, "Nancy, you and Bess and George have done such a wonderful job so far in solving the Sunnymead mystery, I want you to take over the final part. I suggest that you three and Ned, Burt, and Dave go with Captain Runcie to the *River Princess*. He will see what he can do about moving it."

The girls were delighted with this arrangement and three canoes were brought to the dock. Nancy and Ned stepped into the first craft and took Captain Runcie with them   when the group reached the *River Princess*, the towboat owner said he would remain outside and make some calculations.

The three girls began showing their escorts around the showboat. Ned, poking into various crannies with his flashlight, said laughingly, "I'm not going to give up until I find that pirate treasure."

In their search he and Nancy finally reached the hold of the old vessel. Walking on the dry part, they beamed the light back and forth.

Suddenly Nancy stooped down and said, "Ned, here's something interesting I missed before. They may be a clue." She pointed to a series of knotholes on one of the wide boards in the center of the deck.

"But this isn't under a bulkhead, as the legend said," Ned objected.

Nancy smiled. "Those pirates were clever. Do you realize we're standing under a bulkhead of the theater on the upper deck? Ned, let's try lifting up this board."

"Okay. But with what?" Ned asked, looking about.

Not far away Nancy spotted a crowbar which she had seen Charles use the day she had visited the boat the first time. Ned hurried to pick it up, then started to pry up the section of floor.

Nancy waited breathlessly. Would her hunch

pay off? Suddenly, with a ripping sound, the floor board came up.

"Oh!" she exclaimed excitedly.

Beneath the board was another board, old and rotted, and below this, a metal chest!

Nancy and Ned, after a few tugs, lifted the lid, revealing a mass of gold coins!

"We've found it! We've found it!" Ned cried out. He ran his hand through the coins. "There must be fifty thousand dollars' worth!"

As he and Nancy did a little dance together to express their glee, they were completely unaware of two sinister figures who suddenly arose from behind a pile of crates and rags nearby. The two men held stout sticks in their hands. Quietly and stealthily they leaped toward the couple and brought the sticks down full force on their heads. Nancy and Ned slumped to the deck.

Above, Bess and Dave were just completing a tour of the first deck. A few minutes later they came toward the entrance to the hold. Bess suddenly yelled in alarm:

"Smoke's coming from the hold. The showboat's on fire! Nancy and Ned are down there!"

CHAPTER XX

A Masquerader Unmasked

FEARFUL that Nancy and Ned were trapped in the hold of the *River Princess,* Bess cried out their names in terror. There was no answer.

"We must do something!" the girl wailed.

At this instant George and Burt arrived. Quickly Bess and Dave told them of their fears for Nancy and Ned. The two boys tied handkerchiefs over their noses and mouths, turned on their flashlights, and rushed down the steps. Reaching the smoke-filled hold, Burt and Dave peered around frantically.

"There they are—over there!" Burt pointed.

Nancy and Ned lay on the floor, unconscious. Quickly the two boys swung the prostrate forms over their shoulders, covered Nancy's and Ned's mouths and noses with their hands, and dashed up the steps. The injured couple were laid on the deck.

Bess knelt down beside them. "See those lumps on their heads! They've been hit."

As George and Bess began to try reviving their friends, Burt, Dave, and Captain Runcie grabbed fire buckets still hanging on the deck and rushed down into the hold.

"Oh, do be careful!" Bess called after them.

In a few minutes Nancy and Ned regained consciousness. Both sat up and asked groggily, "What happened?"

Bess said someone must have knocked them out in the hold. "And there's a fire down there, too. Do you know anything about it?"

"We didn't see any fire," Ned replied.

Down in the hold, Captain Runcie and his two companions were busily sloshing water from the listed side of the deck onto the burning section. In a short time they had the flames out. When they returned, Dave asked Nancy and Ned how they felt. Reassured they would be all right, he asked if the couple had seen anyone in the hold.

"No," they replied. Then suddenly Nancy said, "The treasure—is it still there?"

"Treasure!" Dave repeated.

"It was an authentic pirate chest filled with old gold coins," Ned explained. "We found it in the hold."

"Then whoever knocked you out must have stolen it!" declared Burt. "We didn't see a chest."

No one had seen any strangers leave the showboat and so much time had elapsed since the attack that the group knew it would be futile to try finding Nancy and Ned's assailant.

"He must have set the fire, then run up the stairs, and got away when no one was looking," said George.

To make sure he was not still aboard, a careful search was made. The thief, or thieves, had vanished!

"We must return to Sunnymead and report this to the police at once," Nancy decided.

As Captain Runcie and the young people were about to leave the *River Princess*, the gentle sound of paddles came from two directions. In a few moments they saw Charles Bartolome approaching from one entrance to the pond, Uncle Rufus from another. The new arrivals were amazed to hear what had taken place on the showboat.

"I'm sorry that you two were hurt," said Charles grimly. "So the legend about the pirate treasure *was* true!"

Uncle Rufus said he had news for Nancy. He had seen nothing suspicious at the *River Princess* the evening before. But he had been making some inquiries among his neighbors. One, a Negro boy, had secretly watched two men at work in the showboat late one night. The younger man had carried tools, the other a "talkin' ma-

chine with records." While there, they had played
tom-tom and calliope records. "They also
played some hymns," Uncle Rufus added. "The
men called each other Alex and Spike."

"Not Alex Upgrove?" Charles asked.

Bess motioned the young man aside and
quickly told him the unfortunate story and
their further suspicions about Alex. Charles's
face became grave, and he said softly, "I'm sorry
for Donna Mae."

"She's just crushed," Bess told him. "She real-
izes how foolish she was to think that she was
in love with Alex." Bess smiled. "You know,
Charles, despite what you may think, Donna
Mae has always been very fond of you." Charles
looked thoughtful, but made no reply.

As Bess turned back to the others, she heard
Uncle Rufus say that he thought Spike was hiding out in an empty shack in the bayou.

"Let's go get him!" Ned urged.

Captain Runcie insisted upon going along. But
he added, "I'm much older than the rest of
you and I offer this advice. Girls, don't go on
this man hunt. Those fellows are too dangerous." Nancy reluctantly conceded that he was
right.

Being familiar now with the bayou, the three
girls set off alone in one of the canoes to return
to Sunnymead. When they told their story,
the Havers were astounded. While the group

were excitedly discussing the new developments, Captain Runcie and the Emerson boys returned.

"We caught one of the men!" Dave announced. "But the other one got away with the pirate chest just before we arrived."

Ned said that the man they had caught was Spike Lander, who had many aliases. They had driven him to police headquarters and he was now in jail. If he had any idea where Alex had gone with the pirate gold, he had refused to admit it. But the Louisiana police and those of Mississippi and other adjoining states had been alerted.

"Alex ought to be caught soon," Ned prophesied.

Colonel Haver said he certainly hoped so. Then, turning to Captain Runcie, he asked about the possibility of moving the showboat to the Sunnymead dock.

"I can move the *River Princess* with very little trouble," the captain stated. "I'll get men to clear out the rest of the stream and fetch that showboat down here in no time."

Two days went by and still there was no word of Alex. Spike Lander had confessed to stealing Nancy's convertible. As the young detective had suspected, he had attempted by several sinister methods to keep her from coming to New Orleans. Other than that he would tell nothing.

"I wish I knew where Alex is," Nancy fretted.

The battered showboat had been hauled to the Havers' dock. Since carpenters and painters of the area were busy on Mardi Gras floats and grandstands, none were available to repair the *River Princess*. Everyone at Sunnymead offered to help.

"I'll accept it," said Colonel Haver gratefully.

Charles heard about the plan and came over to help, bringing Frank and Jack. Hammers, saws, and paintbrushes were kept in use from morning until night.

The *River Princess* would be restored and ready for the grand ball!

Another kind of change was also taking place. Bess, in particular, was thrilled to see Donna Mae and Charles working side by side, talking and laughing. He seemed to have forgotten his hurt feelings and became more and more attentive to his former fiancée each day.

"Oh, I do hope they'll get married," Bess sighed audibly.

At last the *River Princess* was completely restored. The theater was ready for the play. The large room on the upper deck and all the decks were spick-and-span and waxed for dancing. Only the hold would be barred to visitors.

Mrs. Haver remarked, with a pleased smile, "The *Princess* looks simply beautiful. I shall be so happy to have our friends see her."

Colonel Haver thanked everyone as he gazed

proudly at the showboat, then said, "From now on no more work! I want everyone to get into the carnival spirit. Tomorrow evening Mardi Gras week officially begins. I have grandstand seats for the parades."

Nancy and her friends were glad to turn their thoughts to the colorful spectacle. But Nancy still could not get Alex Upgrove out of her mind. Just before leaving for the first parade, she phoned the police, only to be told there was not a clue to the young man's whereabouts.

"If you get any leads, Miss Drew, let us know," the captain requested.

The Havers and their visitors hurried off to New Orleans and found places in the mayor's grandstand. Soon they heard band music, and down the street came the long line of floats.

"It's just like being in fairyland!" Bess exclaimed after several gorgeous floats had passed, lighted by torchbearers running alongside them.

High above the street rolled the glittering imitation gardens, palaces, scenes from mythology, Indian history, Nature, ships, and the sea.

Silks, satins, and velvets were used in profusion in costume and decoration. Every float sparkled with gold or silver posts and canopies.

On the pavement below them crowds of people clapped and cried out for souvenirs. Thousands of imitation pearl necklaces were tossed by the actors into the upturned hands.

"Oh, isn't this the most exciting thing you've ever seen?" Bess asked Nancy as she caught one of the necklaces on the third night of the parades.

"It's simply gorgeous," Nancy agreed.

"Absolutely super!" added George.

Bands were plentiful and high-stepping drum majorettes led by baton twirlers kept up a lively pace behind the musicians.

During all this time Nancy had not forgotten Alex Upgrove. She had remained alert for any clue to him among the vast crowd of people. But night after night went by without a sign of him.

Finally came Shrove Tuesday, the final day of the Mardi Gras celebration. As soon as breakfast was over at Sunnymead, the entire Haver family and their guests donned costumes in preparation for joining the revelers in New Orleans. Today the parade would start at ten-thirty.

As the girls from River Heights and the Emerson boys, all dressed as clowns, rode toward the city in Nancy's car, she said, "I have a hunch. Maybe it's farfetched, but I feel that we'll find Alex Upgrove today."

"How?" Ned asked. "Even if he's around—which I doubt—he'll probably be in costume. That would be the easiest way for him to hide his identity."

"I know that," Nancy answered. "But he hasn't been caught, so I believe he's in town. I can't get that wadded piece of paper out of my mind. I mean the one Alex threw from the car. On it was a patch of maroon with a gold stripe running through the center. It might have meant a float covered by maroon velvet with a gold stripe."

"You mean Alex might be on it?" Ned asked incredulously.

Nancy nodded. "In some way he'll be using the pirate coins." The young detective laughed. "I think Alex might even have made some kind of arrangement to rent the coins to the parade committee, provided he found them before the Mardi Gras. He'll use the cash to get out of town while still in costume."

"And leave the chest of pirate money behind?" Burt asked unbelievingly.

"Oh, no," said Nancy. "He'll manage to take it with him."

Nancy suggested that since all of them were in similar costumes, it might be wise for them to separate. "If Alex is around, he won't be so apt to notice us. We'll meet you later on where the parade breaks up on Claiborne Avenue."

Ned parked the car and the six masked revelers alighted. He and Nancy found an advantageous spot from which to watch the parade as it went along St. Charles Avenue. Float after float went by without arousing any more than admiration on the part of the young people. Then suddenly Nancy grabbed Ned's arm.

"Look!" she whispered excitedly. "Here comes a pirate float and around the outside is maroon velvet with a gold stripe!"

She and Ned watched intently as the float came closer. Three of the "pirates" were busy throwing necklaces to the costumed revelers in the street below them. A fourth pirate was bent over a treasure chest. He was busy sifting gold coins through his fingers, much to the delight of the crowd.

"Throw me some of your money!" cried a bystander dressed as a knight in armor.

"Yes, I'd like some pirates' money!" called his companion in a skeleton costume.

The cloaked pirate merely laughed. As he passed just above Nancy she peered at him searchingly, trying to figure out what his face would look like without make-up and mustache. After the float had gone by, she whispered excitedly to Ned:

"I think that was Alex. Let's follow him!"

The two kept a short distance behind the float and wound their way in and out among the crowd. By the time they reached Canal Street, where the parade turned, Nancy was positive that the float pirate with the gold coins was Alex Upgrove.

"I'm going to notify the first policeman we see," she told Ned.

"Good idea," he agreed.

Not far away they met an officer and quickly apprised him of their suspicions. He promised to alert headquarters at once, have the pirate float put under surveillance, and the man handling the coins questioned when the parade disbanded.

"I'll be there to identify him," Nancy said.

She and Ned continued to follow the maroon-and-gold float. As it came near the area where the parade would break up, they saw the "pirate" suddenly stuff his many pockets with coins from the treasure chest. The rest he dumped into a small sack he was holding and tucked this into his velvet waistcoat.

"That's Alex, all right," said Nancy. "Oh, Ned, look! He's going to jump off the float and get away before the police come!"

"But he won't get away from me," declared Ned grimly.

The man jumped to the sidewalk. As he started to run, Ned made a flying leap and the two crashed to the pavement.

Several revelers screamed. Their outcries caught the attention of the police who were waiting a short distance away. In a few seconds two officers were on the scene. By this time Ned had pulled the "pirate" to his feet and was holding him in a viselike grip.

Nancy rushed up and definitely identified the suspect as Alex Upgrove. His hat, wig, and mustache had fallen off in the struggle and most of his make-up had rubbed away.

"What's the meaning of this?" Alex asked angrily.

"You're under arrest," said one of the officers.

"I haven't done anything wrong," the fugitive contended stoutly.

"According to this young lady, you have several crimes to your credit."

The officer named only one—knocking out Ned and Nancy on the showboat and setting the fire. On hearing this, Alex broke down and confessed that Alex Upgrove was not his right name, although he refused to say who he was. Months before the Mardi Gras, he had met Spike Lander, who had heard the rumor of the pirate coins.

"Spike needed somebody with class to ingratiate himself with the Havers and keep track of what was going on, so he chose me. I figured out this Oxford business and it worked all right with Donna Mae and her parents. But you, Nancy Drew, spoiled the whole game."

Alex admitted that he and Spike had arranged to haunt the showboat. When Nancy was learning too much, he had followed her to the De la Vernes'. The elderly Oxford graduate had been his undoing.

"So I had to leave Sunnymead," he said. "But Spike and I weren't going to give up hunting for that pirate treasure. When Nancy found it for us, we had to knock her out to escape. The fire was accidental. Spike lighted a match and in the rush to get away I guess he dropped it."

Alex went on to say that he had arranged, also in advance, to be included as a pirate on the float under still another important assumed name. He had figured if all went well he could use it as a surprise for Donna Mae, whom he really had intended to marry and gain a social position for himself.

At this, Nancy and Ned exchanged glances as if to say, "What tremendous conceit the man has, to believe he could have gotten away permanently with such a scheme!"

Alex had also figured that if his plans went wrong, Mardi Gras Day would be an excellent one in which to disappear. As Nancy had guessed, he had rented the coins to the parade committee and planned to use the cash to make a getaway.

She had also been right about the wad of paper, with the identifying maroon and gold. It had been a signal to Spike. There was invisible writing on it, asking his partner to help trail Nancy.

"Yes, Spike rigged that vine barricade," Alex admitted when Nancy questioned him on this. "And he and I used a duck call to signal each other whenever he thought anyone else was in the vicinity of the showboat."

"And did he throw the stone at me and play ghost on the *River Princess?*"

"Yes."

When the captive's story was finished, the police officer said to him, "Well, Upgrove, your masquerade has ended. Your pal is behind bars and that's where you're going, also. It's too bad you chose the wrong kind of company when you got along so well with nice folks."

Bess, George, and their companions reached the group just then. Nancy said, "Alex has confessed," and the prisoner was led away.

"Well, Nancy, you solved the mystery of the haunted showboat and did a magnificent job," Ned praised her.

"Hip-hip-hurray!" said Burt, striking an exaggerated pose.

Nancy laughed. "Now that the mystery is solved, let's have some fun." But suddenly a wistful feeling came over her as she thought, "When will I have a chance to solve another?"

Nancy's question was to be answered very soon, when she found herself involved in *The Secret of the Golden Pavilion.*

In a gay mood the young people returned home. Their hosts and Donna Mae were already there. With them was Charles. All listened in awe and admiration as Bess and George told about the capture of the false Alex Upgrove and the recovery of the pirate treasure.

"It's unbelievable," said Colonel Haver. "Nancy, how can we ever thank you? Unless," he added, a twinkle in his eyes, "the pirate treasure you found is reward enough."

Nancy stared in amazement. "Oh, I shan't claim that! I'd like one coin as a souvenir, but you and the De la Vernes should share the treasure."

"We'll see," said Colonel Haver. There was silence for a few moments, then he continued. "Nancy, you are responsible for something far more important than solving the mystery of the haunted showboat. I want to take this opportunity to tell you all that after the pageant tonight, the engagement of my daughter Donna Mae to Charles Bartolome will be formally announced."

"Oh, I'm so happy to hear that!" Nancy cried out, and Bess and George gave a rousing cheer.

Donna Mae hugged Nancy gratefully and on her cheek the young detective could feel a few tears.

"Nancy, you helped me recover something more precious than all the gold in the world," Donna Mae whispered.

Order Form
New revised editions of
THE BOBBSEY TWINS®

In *hardcover* at your local bookseller OR
simply mail in this handy order coupon and start your collection today!

Please send me the following Bobbsey Twins titles I've checked below.

AVOID DELAYS   Please Print Order Form Clearly

❏ 1	Of Lakeport	($5.99)	448-09071-6
❏ 2	Adventure in the Country	($5.95)	448-09072-4
❏ 6	On a Houseboat	($4.95)	448-09099-6
❏ 7	Mystery at Meadowbrook	($4.50)	448-09100-3
❏ 8	Big Adventure at Home	($4.50)	448-09134-8

Own the original exciting
BOBBSEY TWINS® ADVENTURE STORIES
still available:

❏13	Visit to the Great West	($4.50)	448-08013-3

**VISIT PUTNAM BERKLEY ONLINE
ON THE INTERNET: http://www.putnam.com/berkley**

Payable in U.S. funds. No cash accepted. Postage & handling: $3.50 for one book. $1.00 for each additional. Maximum postage $8.50. Prices, postage and handling charges may change without notice. Visa, Amex, MasterCard call 1-800-788-6262, ext. 1, or fax 1-201-933-2316.

Or, check above books
and send this order form to:

**The Putnam Publishing Group
P.O. Box 12289, Dept. B
Newark, NJ 07101-5289**

Please allow 4-6 weeks for delivery.
Foreign and Canadian delivery 8-12 weeks

Book Total $ _____

Applicable Sales Tax $ _____
(CA, NJ, NY, GST Can.)

Postage & Handling $ _____

Total Amount Due $ _____

The Bobbsey Twins® Series is a trademark
of Simon & Schuster, Inc. and is registered
in the United States Patent and Trademark Office.

Bill my: ❏ Visa ❏ MasterCard ❏ Amex _____ (expires)

Card#_____
                                    ($10 minimum)

Daytime Phone # _____

Signature_____

Or enclosed is my: ❏ check ❏ money order
SHIP TO:
Name _____
Address _____
City _____ State _____ Zip _____

BILL TO:
Name _____
Address _____
City _____ State _____ Zip _____

Order Form
Own the original 58 action-packed
HARDY BOYS MYSTERY STORIES®

In *hardcover* at your local bookseller OR
simply mail in this handy order coupon and start your collection today!

Please send me the following Hardy Boys titles I've checked below.
All Books Priced @ $5.99

AVOID DELAYS   Please Print Order Form Clearly

❑	1 Tower Treasure	448-08901-7	❑	30 Wailing Siren Mystery	448-08930-0
❑	2 House on the Cliff	448-08902-5	❑	31 Secret of Wildcat Swamp	448-08931-9
❑	3 Secret of the Old Mill	448-08903-3	❑	32 Crisscross Shadow	448-08932-7
❑	4 Missing Chums	448-08904-1	❑	33 The Yellow Feather Mystery	448-08933-5
❑	5 Hunting for Hidden Gold	448-08905-X	❑	34 The Hooded Hawk Mystery	448-08934-3
❑	6 Shore Road Mystery	448-08906-8	❑	35 The Clue in the Embers	448-08935-1
❑	7 Secret of the Caves	448-08907-6	❑	36 The Secret of Pirates Hill	448-08936-X
❑	8 Mystery of Cabin Island	448-08908-4	❑	37 Ghost at Skeleton Rock	448-08937-8
❑	9 Great Airport Mystery	448-08909-2	❑	38 Mystery at Devil's Paw	448-08938-6
❑	10 What Happened at Midnight	448-08910-6	❑	39 Mystery of the Chinese Junk	448-08939-4
❑	11 While the Clock Ticked	448-08911-4	❑	40 Mystery of the Desert Giant	448-08940-8
❑	12 Footprints Under the Window	448-08912-2	❑	41 Clue of the Screeching Owl	448-08941-6
❑	13 Mark on the Door	448-08913-0	❑	42 Viking Symbol Mystery	448-08942-4
❑	14 Hidden Harbor Mystery	448-08914-9	❑	43 Mystery of the Aztec Warrior	448-08943-2
❑	15 Sinister Sign Post	448-08915-7	❑	44 The Haunted Fort	448-08944-0
❑	16 A Figure in Hiding	448-08916-5	❑	45 Mystery of the Spiral Bridge	448-08945-9
❑	17 Secret Warning	448-08917-3	❑	46 Secret Agent on Flight 101	448-08946-7
❑	18 Twisted Claw	448-08918-1	❑	47 Mystery of the Whale Tattoo	448-08947-5
❑	19 Disappearing Floor	448-08919-X	❑	48 The Arctic Patrol Mystery	448-08948-3
❑	20 Mystery of the Flying Express	448-08920-3	❑	49 The Bombay Boomerang	448-08949-1
❑	21 The Clue of the Broken Blade	448-08921-1	❑	50 Danger on Vampire Trail	448-08950-5
❑	22 The Flickering Torch Mystery	448-08922-X	❑	51 The Masked Monkey	448-08951-3
❑	23 Melted Coins	448-08923-8	❑	52 The Shattered Helmet	448-08952-1
❑	24 Short-Wave Mystery	448-08924-6	❑	53 The Clue of the Hissing Serpent	448-08953-X
❑	25 Secret Panel	448-08925-4	❑	54 The Mysterious Caravan	448-08954-8
❑	26 The Phantom Freighter	448-08926-2	❑	55 The Witchmaster's Key	448-08955-6
❑	27 Secret of Skull Mountain	448-08927-0	❑	56 The Jungle Pyramid	448-08956-4
❑	28 The Sign of the Crooked Arrow	448-08928-9	❑	57 The Firebird Rocket	448-08957-2
❑	29 The Secret of the Lost Tunnel	448-08929-7	❑	58 The Sting of the Scorpion	448-08958-0

Also Available The Hardy Boys Detective Handbook 448-01990-6

VISIT PUTNAM BERKLEY ONLINE
ON THE INTERNET: http://www.putnam.com/berkley

Payable in U.S. funds. No cash accepted. Postage & handling: $3.50 for one book. $1.00 for each additional. Maximum postage $8.50. Prices, postage and handling charges may change without notice. Visa, Amex, MasterCard call 1-800-788-6262, ext. 1, or fax 1-201-933-2316.

Or, check above books
and send this order form to:

**The Putnam Publishing Group
P.O. Box 12289, Dept. B
Newark, NJ 07101-5289**

Bill my: ❑ Visa ❑ MasterCard ❑ Amex _____ (expires)

Card#_____
($10 minimum)

Daytime Phone # _____

Signature_____

Please allow 4-6 weeks for delivery.
Foreign and Canadian delivery 8-12 weeks

Or enclosed is my: ❑ check ❑ money order
SHIP TO:
Name _____
Address _____
City _____ State _____ Zip _____

Book Total $ _____

Applicable Sales Tax $ _____
(CA, NJ, NY, GST Can.)

Postage & Handling $ _____

Total Amount Due $ _____

BILL TO:
Name _____

Nancy Drew® and The Hardy Boys® are trademarks of Simon & Schuster, Inc. and are registered in the United States Patent and Trademark Office.

Address _____
City _____ State _____ Zip _____

Order Form
Own the original 56 thrilling
NANCY DREW MYSTERY STORIES®

In *hardcover* at your local bookseller OR
simply mail in this handy order coupon and start your collection today!

Please send me the following Nancy Drew titles I've checked below.
All Books Priced @ $5.99

AVOID DELAYS   Please Print Order Form Clearly

☐	1	Secret of the Old Clock	448-09501-7	☐ 30	Clue of the Velvet Mask	448-09530-0
☐	2	Hidden Staircase	448-09502-5	☐ 31	Ringmaster's Secret	448-09531-9
☐	3	Bungalow Mystery	448-09503-3	☐ 32	Scarlet Slipper Mystery	448-09532-7
☐	4	Mystery at Lilac Inn	448-09504-1	☐ 33	Witch Tree Symbol	448-09533-5
☐	5	Secret of Shadow Ranch	448-09505-X	☐ 34	Hidden Window Mystery	448-09534-3
☐	6	Secret of Red Gate Farm	448-09506-8	☐ 35	Haunted Showboat	448-09535-1
☐	7	Clue in the Diary	448-09507-6	☐ 36	Secret of the Golden Pavilion	448-09536-X
☐	8	Nancy's Mysterious Letter	448-09508-4	☐ 37	Clue in the Old Stagecoach	448-09537-8
☐	9	The Sign of the Twisted Candles	448-09509-2	☐ 38	Mystery of the Fire Dragon	448-09538-6
☐	10	Password to Larkspur Lane	448-09510-6	☐ 39	Clue of the Dancing Puppet	448-09539-4
☐	11	Clue of the Broken Locket	448-09511-4	☐ 40	Moonstone Castle Mystery	448-09540-8
☐	12	The Message in the Hollow Oak	448-09512-2	☐ 41	Clue of the Whistling Bagpipes	448-09541-6
☐	13	Mystery of the Ivory Charm	448-09513-0	☐ 42	Phantom of Pine Hill	448-09542-4
☐	14	The Whispering Statue	448-09514-9	☐ 43	Mystery of the 99 Steps	448-09543-2
☐	15	Haunted Bridge	448-09515-7	☐ 44	Clue in the Crossword Cipher	448-09544-0
☐	16	Clue of the Tapping Heels	448-09516-5	☐ 45	Spider Sapphire Mystery	448-09545-9
☐	17	Mystery of the Brass-Bound Trunk	448-09517-3	☐ 46	The Invisible Intruder	448-09546-7
☐	18	Mystery at Moss-Covered Mansion	448-09518-1	☐ 47	The Mysterious Mannequin	448-09547-5
☐	19	Quest of the Missing Map	448-09519-X	☐ 48	The Crooked Banister	448-09548-3
☐	20	Clue in the Jewel Box	448-09520-3	☐ 49	The Secret of Mirror Bay	448-09549-1
☐	21	The Secret in the Old Attic	448-09521-1	☐ 50	The Double Jinx Mystery	448-09550-5
☐	22	Clue in the Crumbling Wall	448-09522-X	☐ 51	Mystery of the Glowing Eye	448-09551-3
☐	23	Mystery of the Tolling Bell	448-09523-8	☐ 52	The Secret of the Forgotten City	448-09552-1
☐	24	Clue in the Old Album	448-09524-6	☐ 53	The Sky Phantom	448-09553-X
☐	25	Ghost of Blackwood Hall	448-09525-4	☐ 54	The Strange Message	
☐	26	Clue of the Leaning Chimney	448-09526-2		in the Parchment	448-09554-8
☐	27	Secret of the Wooden Lady	448-09527-0	☐ 55	Mystery of Crocodile Island	448-09555-6
☐	28	The Clue of the Black Keys	448-09528-9	☐ 56	The Thirteenth Pearl	448-09556-4
☐	29	Mystery at the Ski Jump	448-09529-7			

VISIT PUTNAM BERKLEY ONLINE
ON THE INTERNET: http://www.putnam.com/berkley

Payable in U.S. funds. No cash accepted. Postage & handling: $3.50 for one book. $1.00 for each additional. Maximum postage $8.50. Prices, postage and handling charges may change without notice. Visa, Amex, MasterCard call 1-800-788-6262, ext. 1, or fax 1-201-933-2316.

Or, check above books
and send this order form to:

**The Putnam Publishing Group
P.O. Box 12289, Dept. B
Newark, NJ 07101-5289**

Please allow 4-6 weeks for delivery.
Foreign and Canadian delivery 8-12 weeks

Bill my: ☐ Visa ☐ MasterCard ☐ Amex _____ (expires)

Card#_____
($10 minimum)

Daytime Phone # _____

Signature_____

Or enclosed is my: ☐ check ☐ money order
SHIP TO:

Book Total	$ _____	Name _____
Applicable Sales Tax	$ _____	Address _____
(CA, NJ, NY, GST Can.)		City _____ State _____ Zip _____
Postage & Handling	$ _____	**BILL TO:**
Total Amount Due	$ _____	Name _____

Nancy Drew® and The Hardy Boys® are trademarks of Simon & Schuster, Inc. and are registered in the United States Patent and Trademark Office.

Address _____

City _____ State _____ Zip _____